How Witches

Get their Broomsticks

The Gathering

By

John McIntyre

Acknowledgement

Illustrations by CTC Photography, exclusively for *How Witches Get Their Broomsticks: The Gathering*. All rights reserved to this book.

Western Publishing House

James, Eric Silva, and the entire team, for taking this manuscript and shaping it into the best it could possibly be.

Book Publishing and Audiobook Publishing by

Western Publishing House

(www.westernpublishinghouse.com)

The help and guidance I needed to navigate the publishing world has been made an easy task by those kind and generous people. They have made my work as a writer and creator a better and more fulfilling experience.

I hope I have made the correct decision to self-publish and to use the experienced teams available, in order to provide the readers of my work with the very best and most satisfying reading or audio experience possible.

Not many books include in the acknowledgements the readers themselves, but I must say just how fantastic it is for an author to know that they have chosen to read my work. I am, and always will be, grateful that you have allowed me to bring this story to you, and I hope you enjoy this book as much as I loved writing it.

So, to you, the reader, my thanks.

John McIntyre

Dedication

Val and my family.

Paula, her partner Gordon, and my granddaughter Grace, and of course not forgetting the next small addition to this wonderful family due in just a wee while. Clare and her partner Thomas, and everyone's favourite, Mady, my ever-crazy border collie.

Heather, just for being my favourite cousin, and her two fantastic daughters.

Nicole is the very first Val Witch to appear in *How Witches Get Their Broomsticks*, along with her cat Zeus.

Natalie kindly gave me her photo to use as Val Witch in *How Witches Get Their Broomsticks: The Gathering*.

Koreen gave help on both books in selling and guidance. She is expecting in October this year and I cannot wait to see the little one.

To be honest, I could sit and tell you of the help and support from my entire family, and truly I am blessed. They gather around and give confidence and support, very quick to judge but even faster to lift you up high. Their love and support inspire me to always keep going and be better.

My wife and my family, who see me at my best and of course my worst. To say I love you all is the easiest thing for me to write.

Colin Tinsley

A dear friend who gave me hope and told me, "Forget the past and get inspired, I will help, old friend." Sadly, he passed away, but his wife Sonia continues to remind me, whenever I have doubts, to remember and complete. Colin was so flaming proud of my writing and of me following my dreams. I must admit a wee tear comes when I think of some of the things we got up to playing rugby and drinking far too much, but these are now the legendary stories that are not for telling in books, but for sharing while sitting around with a nice whisky, or whatever, and taking a wee while just to remember.

Friends are just someone you have not said hello to yet, so spend your life saying hello to as many as you can. You will be all the better for it.

About the author

This is a little bit about me, the author of *How Witches Get Their Broomsticks*, *How Witches Get Their Broomsticks: The Gathering*, and *Floss the Dancing Dinosaur*.

I never really intended to write, let alone manage to have three books published, but the journey to bring the characters and creations of those books to you all has been great fun. I was encouraged by my good friend Colin Tinsley, who persuaded me to share the book that I had once taken on holiday to the Polish city of Kraków. On a quiet night I asked his son Callum to read the very rough copy of *How Witches Get Their Broomsticks*, which he did to everyone in the room. And so, on that day, we reached the conclusion: why not try and have this published?

The timeline, from this short story being written while sitting in bed with my wife Val, has been long, and at times the overwhelming feeling of wanting to give up brought back anxieties from my time spent at Dunblane Primary and High School in Dunblane, Scotland. Sport I loved, and even going to school to be with friends was great, but English was hard work for me and created a real sense of hatred. I did not like the whole experience at all, though I enjoyed creating stories. It has always been there, but as many older people will remember, reading and writing was a battle if you were slow to pick it up. For both the teaching staff and me, it made school horrible.

Over time I learnt to overcome what I could not do by working around the problem throughout my life. I suppose having a good friend push me in the right direction to rebuild my confidence after so many years has brought a joy to my life that I never saw coming.

I now drive large artic trucks long distances, and writing is a passion that I love sharing. From a trainee welder to windscreen and sunroof glass installer and manager, to a chef and bar person, I can say my life has been both fun and rewarding. I even worked at McDonald's. Looking back, the people and experiences have brought me more joy than I could ever express. I guess the more people in your life the better.

I have always loved hearing about people and their lives, but more than anything, getting stuck into new things or trying to better myself. Not always for money, but mostly just because. I am now 57 years old, and have been through two marriages in which I would have to say the fault for failure firmly lay with me. I simply worked too hard. But the experiences I now have from my partners have been extraordinary.

The foster caring gave me so much more than I could ever give back. Each and every one of those children taught me more about life than I could ever have known. They have left me proud of them, and always wishing I could have done more.

I was not blessed with children of my own, but I have been a stepfather to four, and I hope I have been a good one. I always remember my own father Ian McIntyre's words of advice: "Always be kind and generous, and when it goes wrong, which it will, be the one to comfort." He was of course right. A lot goes wrong in life, but being picked up by the ones you love and encouraged, whether or not you are their real dad or mum, gives the mental stability needed in what is, at times, a very cruel world.

Now I watch this world and the hard times faced by ordinary people everywhere. My heart is saddened by these times, but I remain positive that they will change and get better. To only look at the sad things will bring your mental wellbeing to a point of instability. That is why media overload makes you sad.

I hope my book brings a small moment of reflection and joy.

Yours with love, from Dundee, Scotland,

John McIntyre

Val Witch

Introduction

We join Val and Magnificent the cat after the triumph of Val managing to invent Rodney the broomstick, along with thousands of other broomsticks that can fly. Eagerly, they are awaiting the invite to the Great Gathering. Some were a wee bit more excited than others.

This was a special day that Val had worked so hard for. Her dreams and hopes would all be realised if she was given this invite. The ceremony would take place at the Great Castle on the Isle of Skye, during a massive Inaugural Ball where the nominated would, if lucky, be inducted into the Witches Council. And, of course, the Witch of the Year would be chosen by the Boss.

Of course, nothing was going to go according to plan.

Chapter 1
Flight School.

Rodney, Val Witch's ever-lovable broomstick, had some quite peculiar flying habits. Some might even say a little dangerous. To put it as politely as possible, the only good description would be unbelievably frightening. Val's ever-loyal furry friend, Magnificent, had other ways of describing Rodney's behaviour. However, we cannot repeat them. So, it was decided, after much consideration, that the best thing to do would be to try and teach Rodney to fly better for everyone's safety.

We join Val and Magnificent as Val reminds everyone that, once again, it was time to take out Rodney for another flying lesson. Rodney was very excited and was pacing backwards and forwards outside.

Of course, Magnificent was lying in his happiest place beside the fire, ensuring that he was toasting himself as efficiently as possible. Magnificent liked to think that he had perfected the correct fur-to-burn ratio. No one likes to have burnt fur – the smell is just disgusting.

Stirring, he remarked, "Rodney is just too high-spirited." He stretched out, continuing, "We will never manage to teach that broomstick anything." Magnificent rolled over to ensure every single part of his old fur was being evenly toasted to perfection.

Val was now trying her best to stir this old cat into some kind of action, hoping for some help, to be honest. She was not keen on the idea of flying alone and was hoping that her cat would come along. It was going to be difficult, as Rodney had crashed a few times and Magnificent was now terrified of flying.

She asked softly that the grumpy old cat come along, trying to remind Magnificent that the agreement was they were all to help.

"You, my little grumpy one, have made an agreement with me," Val stated, reminding the cat that an agreement with a witch was something you should think about very carefully before breaking. Val resisted using threats, but tried the self-preservation approach.

"Magnificent," Val asked quietly, "have you forgotten the feeling of landing on your head, then flying freestyle towards being smashed into the barn?" She hoped this would make Magnificent understand the importance of those flying lessons, hoping the grumpy old cat would encourage Rodney.

Gently yawning, Magnificent looked towards Val, then explained to his very own witch, "Not bothered. I have reached the conclusion that walking might well be the best option for me. Flying is just not safe enough yet, my sweet Val."

Sensing that Val was a little upset, Magnificent went on, "Maybe if it comes with table service, reclining seats and my very own cosy spot, I might consider it."

Val Witch turned to Magnificent, absolutely boiling at this whole situation, but understanding that it was completely wrong to make someone do something against their will. How do you ask someone to risk life and limb on a flying broomstick?

Now trying to balance the right amount of anger with politeness, and without being too aggressive, Val shouted, "You are helping – you must! It wouldn't be the same without a little Magnificent on board." She was trying to be as charming as possible, realising there was no way Magnificent would do anything if he did not wish to.

A small nod from the cat seemed to indicate that the argument was over, but let's not pretend this stubborn cat would give in that easily.

Val was a little upset at having been so annoyed with Magnificent, understanding why he was so scared. She decided to get something to help the cat feel safer while flying: a little flying jacket with matching goggles and, best of all, a crash helmet with *No Fear* written on the front and *This Way Up* written on the back.

Magnificent is going to love this, Val thought, as the order was placed with *Wishing You Had It All Company*. She ticked the box marked *Get It to Me Now*. Within four minutes, it had been delivered.

Three doors down in Fortingall, someone had started this business, and it turned out that little flying jackets with matching goggles and helmets for cats had become popular with the growing sales of broomsticks.

"Thank you!" shouted a cheerful delivery person who had just thrown the package through the front window.

Val screamed words that we are far too polite to repeat.

"Magnificent, my little furry friend," Val called out, still on a charm offensive and trying to entice Magnificent to come and see what had been purchased for him.

Magnificent responded, dragging himself from the cosy fire. Val opened the box, showing its contents, and said that all the cats were wearing them. "You're going to feel so much safer with them on, my furry friend."

Magnificent put them on, and he liked them. He did, of course, look completely ridiculous, but Val was happy that Magnificent was happy and so said nothing. Once again, it looked like the cottage had returned to a tranquil happiness.

Val now watched as Magnificent carefully moved paperwork around. He opened his most secretive place and told Val not to look.

"What are you up to now?" she asked inquisitively.

"Well," Magnificent said proudly, "it's my Last Will and Testament. Got it from the lawyers down the road. They told me that ever since you crazy witches have started flying, they have never been so busy."

"That will be the same bunch who are always trying to sue me!" Val exclaimed. "They are always claiming it's down to us every time something goes wrong with broomsticks. I've told them at least three times that we advise the broomsticks are of their own free will, therefore it's not our fault if something goes wrong."

"That's the very ones," Magnificent said proudly.

All the efforts Val had put into persuading Magnificent seemed to be paying off, as it looked like the cat was now fine with helping to teach Rodney the broomstick to fly.

"Thank goodness," Val thought. "It would have been so much harder without the cat."

And so, Val decided that it was now time to take to the night skies once again. Best of all, it was a full moon tonight. Looking towards the cat, Val cheerfully called out, "Okay, Magnificent. Are we ready for our adventure tonight? We will once again try to teach Rodney. You up for this, my old furry friend?"

She tried to sound as confident as possible. Val knew that very quickly this situation could turn very bad. She hoped that by being as nice as possible to Magnificent, this most stubborn cat would put on his safety gear and all would be well, and they would take to the night skies.

This happy thought was about to come unstuck.

The scene in the cottage descended into utter chaos. Val chased Magnificent.

"You are going!" Val pleaded. "Come on, put your new flying jacket on."

"No way!" came the reply from Magnificent. "That broomstick's only fit for the fire."

"Your helmet is over there by the door, and don't forget your goggles," Val told this most grumpy cat. "And you are going!" Val exclaimed.

"No way!" this most stubborn cat screamed back.

Poor Magnificent was far from convinced that flying was for him, and certainly not on a broomstick whose mission in life seemed to be to hurt a small, defenceless cat. Tearing back to his most favourite spot, Magnificent refused to go.

"I will come in a few moments," the terrified cat tried to negotiate with Val.

Val pulled at Magnificent, trying to stop this stubborn old cat from heading back to his cosy spot. Sounds of the cat's claws scraping across the wooden floor could be heard even outside the cottage.

Then, standing at the door, Rodney the broomstick spoke, pleading with Magnificent that it would not be the same without him.

"I will think about it," Magnificent told them both.

Rodney then said to the terrified cat, "You will enjoy tonight. I promise to do the very best flying ever."

"Come on now," Val pleaded. "You have your new flying jacket and goggles. Just sit on Rodney – it's going to be okay."

Val and Rodney now had to wait for Magnificent to decide whether he would put on the flying jacket.

"But first, a small nap," Magnificent announced. "Then I will let you know."

Much to their surprise, the flying jacket was put on as the cat went for a nap. Within a few moments, this most stubborn one had fallen fast asleep, still wearing his flying jacket.

"Look," Val told Rodney, "we must seize this opportunity while old grumpy is sleeping."

Val gently picked him up and placed him onto Rodney. "Move slowly outside – don't wake Magnificent," she told the broomstick.

Rodney gently moved outside, followed by Val carrying a cute little crash helmet.

"Right," Val said, "prepare for take-off, but wait stealthily until Magnificent is ready. Because if we don't, we will never get him on you again. And it's not fair."

Val gently climbed onto Rodney. "Better pop the helmet on." As she did so, Magnificent let off a loud, smelly fart. It was truly disgusting.

The smell was horrible. Rodney got scared and immediately took off vertically, with Val and Magnificent hanging on for dear life.

"Rodney!" Val demanded. "Fly straight and gently, please. Come on now, we spoke about this."

Magnificent was now screaming as loudly as one small cat could.

"Why?" he screamed. "What on earth is going on? One moment I am sat in my most cosy place and now I am preparing to die! Why, Val, why?"

"You'll be fine," Val tried to reassure him. "Rodney is a good broomstick – look how gently we are flying. Now, Magnificent, we must be sensitive to Rodney's feelings. After all, it was you who caused this to happen – you and that smelly bum."

Vertical take-off was not what anyone would call gentle. Without any warning – just straight up – it was terrifying.

"It wasn't as bad as the smell we left behind us," Val told Magnificent, and once again reminded him, "We must be sensitive to Rodney. You know how easy it is to upset this most sensitive broomstick. Now apologise to Rodney, and we can all have a fun time learning to fly."

Sensing the fear in Val's voice, Magnificent reluctantly mumbled an apology. "Sorry, Rodney – just couldn't help but let a little wind go."

"That's fine," came a reply from Rodney. "Let's fly."

Rodney now started manoeuvres to level off, as all the time they had been arguing they had been heading straight up.

"Rodney," Val now asked, "can we perhaps gently head down?"

"Okay – you are of course in charge," came the reply, and they began to descend towards the ground.

All was now going well about three thousand feet above the Great Caledonian Forest. Magnificent was starting to relax.

"Well, this is not so bad," he shouted to Val, starting to enjoy the flight. "Perhaps you were right," he exclaimed. "Rodney can learn – this is exciting, and it feels safe."

"Right, Rodney, let's try out some simple manoeuvres."

"Great," came the reply. "You tell me, and it shall be done."

"Okay – turn towards the village, gently," Val asked calmly. It happened with no problems at all.

"Okay, Rodney, you are doing well. Now let's just head towards our home," Val asked calmly again.

Rodney once again turned gently, and at this point even Magnificent was impressed.

"Can I do some zig-zags before we get home?" Rodney eagerly asked.

"Okay – but remember, gently," Val said.

Rodney was a teenager, and his coordination was just a wee bit mixed up, shall we say, and the zig-zags were on the scary side.

Now came the big problem. Rodney thought he had spotted Dave the tree and got unbelievably excited.

"Look – down there!" Rodney screamed. "It's Dave! We must go down – he will be so proud of me and all I have learned today."

Without any warning at all, Rodney went into a vertical dive towards Dave the tree.

Val looked towards the ground rushing up at them. Magnificent tightened his crash helmet and shouted at Val that this was all her fault.

"Who ever heard of a cat on a broomstick anyway?" he screamed.

Dave looked up, thinking that for some reason Magnificent was calling out something. He couldn't hear it clearly and it seemed to be coming from the night sky. Night-time can play such tricks in the Great Caledonian Forest – strange noises always seem to echo through it.

Dave - The Tree

Dave still looked to see what it had been, hoping it was not squirrels. Dave was not very fond of them – in fact, he was afraid of them. Still, noises seemed to come and go.

Never mind, Dave thought, and went back to sleep.

Meanwhile, Magnificent and Val were bracing themselves for the inevitable impact.

"Hang on," Val told her beloved cat, while pleading with Rodney, "Slow down, please – come on, please slow."

Rodney then stopped in mid-air, calling out that it was a mistake. "That's not Dave the tree at all – they all look the same in this moonlight."

Magnificent looked at Val. Both quietly breathed a sigh of relief.

Now they were heading back towards the village, grateful they had survived thus far.

Val called to Rodney, "Okay – now try to remember, slow and calm is just beautiful and safe. You can do this."

Magnificent was hanging onto Rodney as tightly as possible. Val was trying her very best to keep Rodney as calm as she could.

Rodney now went as slowly as possible towards the village. In preparation for landing, Val tried to explain what would be best.

"Rodney," Val called softly.

"Yes?" Rodney replied.

"Time to work on those landings," Val reminded him.

Proudly, Rodney gently started to descend ever closer to the village, with all the training now seeming to have made a difference.

It was normally at this point that there was a slight chance of death. This was why Magnificent's thoughts drifted off to think about the future financial well-being and his Last Will and Testament.

Strangely enough, there was now a whole new professional industry specialising in "suing before you fly" that had sprung up in the small village.

Val, at this point on the flight home, would normally encourage Rodney to do his now famous zigzag, with Magnificent on the broomstick providing large amounts of newly cooked lunch to splat over this bunch of most horrible ones as they flew over them.

Val had to admit, this made her day. Even the long-suffering cat, Magnificent, liked this. But they were trying to encourage a new and safer way for Rodney, and so this was not going to happen tonight. Mind you, they weren't promising that it would never happen again.

Fear levels were running very high, largely due to the number of crashes Val and Magnificent had already been subjected to. There was the landing where Rodney had got distracted by a small squirrel smiling. "Oh, how cute," he thought then quickly turned to notice how close the ground was. Other short stories were, of course, available, but my favourite must be Rodney deciding to fly upside down on the approach to the cottage while singing, "How do you like me now?" It took weeks for poor old Magnificent to even speak to Rodney, let alone get back on him.

Encouragement was going to be the key to Rodney becoming the perfect flying broomstick. This was going to take time and patience, and above all, both Val and her long-suffering cat would need to work together. Tonight had been a good night, with only a few things going slightly adrift. Val and Magnificent had decided that the word "wrong" was not to be used, as it was negative.

The time had come to prepare for landing, and Val gave the final instructions.

"Right," Val told Magnificent. "Let's do this cheerfully and as calmly as possible." Hopefully, the Great Caledonian Forest was not going to be once again filled with strange screams and foul language. Tonight, this landing was going to be the best landing ever.

Rodney was excited at the instructions to land. "It's going to be great fun," Rodney exclaimed. Magnificent clung on, closing his eyes and pulling his crash helmet straps tight. Val looked around to see her fearless cat shaking and reciting some kind of last rites.

Up they went to do the final circle around. Val gently reassured them all this was going to be great, with nothing to worry about.

"Okay, Rodney," she said softly. "We're just going to quietly and with care head down towards our landing. Try not to get too excited."

"Magnificent," she asked, "are you okay?"

"Maybe," came a mumbled reply.

Rodney called out the final instructions to the passengers.

"Everyone ready?" he asked.

Rodney then headed into a gentle but controlled... nosedive, with poor old Magnificent screaming and Val shouting. Once again, the forest was filled with the fearful screams of Val and Magnificent.

"I'm very excited!" Rodney screamed.

"Rodney, concentrate on the landing!" Val yelled.

These were the last words before Rodney hit the ground, with Val and her beloved cat flying into the bushes. Magnificent walked off, telling Val, "Not getting on that thing again. It's out to kill us all off."

Rodney looked to be congratulated. "That was much better, was it not?" he asked Val.

No reply came from the bushes, where Val was now trying to set herself free.

"Yes, that was the best yet, I think, Val. Oh, that superb approach drifting in calmly, finding that nearly clear spot as we approached the cottage and barn. And the way I managed to bring us all to a complete stop!" Rodney was now proudly bouncing about, happy at what was, as far as this broomstick was concerned, the best landing ever.

Val, now free from the bushes, looked towards Rodney. "Please, next time do not use the ground as the air brakes. Remember, that's not the way we are now trying to stop just like you did a little while ago. However, you did fantastic tonight. And did you happen to see where Magnificent has gone?"

Chapter 2
The Delivery

'Magnificent!' Val screamed at the top of her voice.

'Come on,' she shouted. 'You are not going to laze about today. Surely you remember what day it is?' she asked her beautiful furry friend.

He replied, hoping she would go away and leave him in peace so he could ensure his whole body was being warmed evenly by the fire. But today was different. Val was not going to let her furry friend laze by the fire. No chance, not today.

'Once again,' she shouted at Magnificent. 'Get up, please. I need to shower and prepare.' She was still trying to emphasise the importance of this day, almost pleading.

'Who cares? It is just another day,' Magnificent replied.

'Now behave. Today is the day.' Val was now rushing about the cottage. 'Wonder what time they will come. Clean up and hurry up about it,' Magnificent was being told.

'Would you get up?' she asked once again of this very grumpy old cat. 'Come on, you know how important it is to me!' Val screamed, still trying to get some kind of interest from Magnificent, who of course cared not one jot.

This was the day that the Great Witches' Council always sent out their invites to The Gathering at the big castle on the Isle of Skye. Her excitement could not be contained. She was running about her house in Fortingall village at full speed, trying to ensure she was ready.

She headed to her shower, telling Magnificent to listen out for the door. 'Make sure to call once the message is in and ready to read out. DO YOU HEAR ME?!'

Magnificent told her of course, and headed back to the cosy open fire. Well, you cannot be too careful when it comes to ensuring your whole body is warmed evenly by the fire. This should never be rushed.

Meanwhile, back in the Great Gathering Council offices, they were making up the final messages.

Colin the clerk shouted, 'Right, time to tell the postal services. Oh, and let us hope we can put the disasters that were the last two Great Gatherings behind us,' reminding all of them of just how lucky they were to escape with their lives. 'Put the messages into the ready-for-collection boxes and hurry up.'

In line with the instructions given by Colin, the messages were placed into the collection boxes. Some were a bit more awkward than others, but they were all eventually ready.

Back at Eagle Courier Service and Postal Service to the Great, Alex, Sandy and Ian were being given the information they needed to collect the messages. Elisabeth, the boss, was busy explaining to her staff that they were to go straight to the destination, no messing around with the messages.

'Under no circumstances will you eat them,' she said, looking directly at Sandy.

He looked down at the ground, trying not to make eye contact. Elisabeth remembered he had done this before, causing chaos when a group of builders did not receive instructions on when to stop building. Three years later, the small shed was now eight storeys high, and the cost was quite unbelievable.

'Do you all understand? Have I made myself clear?' Elisabeth asked, looking at the bunch before her.

'Yes,' they all mumbled.

'Make final preparations for the messages to be delivered and get a move on,' Elisabeth called out to Colin.

'Right.' Alex stepped forward and grabbed the first message. 'Oh, just how cute are you! What is your name?'

He was interrupted by Colin. 'Get a move on, stop playing with the message.'

'Ok,' Alex said. 'I will be on my way.' He turned to his message and looked down at it. 'Oh, you are just the cutest thing. Where are we going? Fortingall, an old place just outside the village of Aberfeldy. You got that? Yes...' Alex replied.

'Right, little one, we head up to the top of the castle ramparts where we shall be preparing for take-off. I will also have to prepare you. Put on safety gear: hat, goggles, and that flying jacket.'

Gerbils got ready but then screamed at the top of his voice. 'Alex!' the message screamed. 'Help me quickly! Help! I have gone blind!' The wee message, nearly in tears, frantically called out.

'Stop,' Alex told him. 'You only have the goggles on back to front, nothing to worry about. Now let me help you.' Alex then put the safety flying goggles on the message, trying to reassure the little one that this was going to be just fine.

'Well, that was an adventure,' Alex told the wee message.

'Yes,' the little message replied.

'Can you be brave?' Alex asked.

'I can be,' the message bravely replied.

Alex gave his nervous passenger a reassuring smile as they made their way to the top of the castle. He climbed up to the ramparts, did final checks, and then leapt off.

Normally I would be telling you of the great, exhilarating feeling that the little message was now experiencing. In all fairness, this is what I should be telling you.

However, Alex had forgotten to seat the message, known as Gerbils, on his back. The wee message was left watching the massive eagle swooping away from the castle. Gerbils was confused and thought perhaps it was now up to him. Of course, that is why it is called a flying jacket.

So he bravely climbed up the last few steps to the top of the ramparts, adjusted his flying goggles, looked out to the vast landscape before him and, closing his eyes, decided to leap off.

Strangely, this little Gerbil's luck was in, as Alex had swooped around the castle after noticing he had no passenger on his back. Just in time, Alex managed to get underneath the falling Gerbil.

'That was close,' Alex told him. 'Why did you jump?'

'Was I not meant to?' Gerbils asked inquisitively.

Smiling, embarrassed but still trying to be professional, Alex replied, 'It is always best to be on my back, as we were both meant to leave at the same time.'

Gerbils was a little confused. Why was it called a flying jacket if you could not fly with it? Still, it had been great fun leaping into the unknown.

Alex, ever the professional, now decided to start a safety announcement.

'We will be flying at about 80 miles per hour and at about eight thousand feet. No in-flight snacks are planned.' Turning to smile at his passenger, he remembered Elisabeth's words: *no eating the message.*

'And may I ask your name?' Alex asked his passenger.

'It is Gerbils the Gerbil,' was the reply.

'I did wonder if that was really your name,' Alex replied. 'Have you ever been flying before, Gerbils?'

'Nope, it is a first for me!'

Alex the eagle...

'Sit back and hang on. It is great fun,' Alex said, turning around to smile at his most nervous passenger.

Alex looked at him and then calmly explained how much better it was with the flying goggles on the right way around. They both laughed. 'Enjoy the flight. Nothing to worry about,' Alex reassured Gerbils.

'That is the spirit, my little cute friend,' Alex added. This big Golden Eagle was now developing a big smile of his own. He could not help but admire the courage of his passenger. One brave creature, jumping from a castle rampart without any way of flying. Alex could feel Gerbils gripping on tightly.

Gerbils - The Mouse

Gerbils had the biggest smile that Alex had ever seen. The little gerbil was completely loving this feeling of flying. It seemed to Alex that this wee gerbil belonged in the air and did not seem to have any fear at all. All that Alex could hear from behind him was:

'Worry not. Let's go faster, go higher, go lower,' Gerbils shouted to Alex.

'You sure about that?' Alex asked.

'Yeah,' Gerbils shouted. 'Come on, let's do it.'

'Hang on then, Gerbils. I am going to dive down,' Alex told him. 'We are going to hit speeds of over 100 miles per hour and skim across the sea.'

Gerbils braced himself as Alex headed into a nosedive. The two of them were completely wrapped up in the experience, every moment reminding Alex just how much he enjoyed this job. But mostly flying. And as for Gerbils, he could not believe this feeling of flying. It was superb.

'Walking is rubbish,' he shouted to Alex. 'Just rubbish. This is the way for me.'

Alex just laughed aloud. 'Yeah, it's the way to go. Anyway, onwards to Fortingall. We have you to deliver, to read the message.'

The whole journey was not going to take long at all. Gerbils had gone from feeling scared to being sad that it would all be over soon.

Alex now flew upwards into the sky towards their destination.

Chapter 3
Tricky Situation

Alex and Gerbils were now about five thousand feet above the village and ready to descend.

'Can you see it?' asked Gerbils.

'Yes,' Alex replied. 'Not long now. Hang on tight, my little friend; we are going to land soon.'

Seconds later, they had landed.

'Right, Gerbils, it's down to you, little fellow. You go make that delivery. I will see you soon,' Alex shouted across to him.

Gerbils approached the door and banged with all his might on it.

Val shouted, 'It's the front door, sleepy cat! Can you open it?'

'No,' Magnificent shouted back.

'Come on, I am in the shower,' Val pleaded. 'Can you just answer it?'

'Ok, I suppose so,' the grumpy old Magnificent reluctantly replied. He made his way to the front door from his most favourite spot beside the warm open fire. He opened the door, looked out, saw nothing, and slammed it shut again before returning to his comfortable spot to relax.

Val shouted again, 'Who was at the front door?'

'Don't know,' Magnificent replied. 'Didn't see a thing. Must have been the wind.'

'Well,' Val shouted, 'the wind is banging again. Now can you get that door and hurry up? Please answer; it might be the message I have been waiting on.'

Magnificent was not happy at having to move from his happy spot once again. He shouted back, 'Okay, I am going,' and dragged his old self off once more.

This time, Gerbils was determined he would get this message delivered. Bang, bang, bang—he bashed as hard as he could.

Finally, his persistence was going to pay off. The door swung open. Magnificent looked down to see little Gerbils standing in front of him.

'Well, would you ever,' Magnificent delightfully smiled, grabbed little Gerbils, and in one bite ate this most unexpected snack. He then went back to his favourite spot to enjoy.

'So?' Val the witch shouted. 'What was at the front door then?'

'Nothing,' came a mumbling reply from Magnificent. 'Just the wind.'

'What did you say?'

'Just the wind,' Magnificent mumbled once again.

'Why are you mumbling?' Val asked. 'Are you snacking again?'

He was unable to reply.

Now the front door was being bashed again, but this time the noise was deafening. Val ran towards the door, which was suddenly forced open. In hopped the biggest eagle she had ever seen. It flew straight past her towards her old cat. The massive eagle then turned Magnificent upside down and threatened that if he did not spit out the message known as Gerbils immediately, the consequences would not be good for an old cat.

Magnificent just opened his mouth, and out dropped his victim. Gerbils lay lifeless on the stone floor.

'What on earth are you doing?' she screamed at Alex, this most angry eagle.

'It's your message that cat has eaten,' came the reply from Alex.

'A message?' Val asked.

'Yes, that's right. He was called Gerbils. He was the bravest and most fearless friend I ever had,' Alex, now with tears flowing from his eyes, replied.

Val asked if she could enquire whether Alex knew what it contained and if it had been from the castle.

'Yes, from the castle,' Alex replied. Val now began to realise what Magnificent had done.

'Do you know what was in the message?'

'How would I know? That silly cat has eaten my friend and I could not care less what the message was,' Alex replied. He was devastated at what had just happened to this hard-working gerbil. He screamed at both Magnificent and Val.

'You're both responsible for his death, and I will be informing the Council of this in my report.'

'Wait, did you say the Witches' Council?' Val asked.

'Yes, that's exactly what I said,' Alex replied. 'Just look at what you two have done. Go on! Look!' he shouted. 'You and that cat.'

'Look at what?' Val replied. 'What has he done?'

Alex then looked around, puzzled. 'Where, just exactly, has Gerbils gone? What trick is this you two are playing?' he demanded. 'Where's Gerbils? Just tell me now.'

Magnificent simply rolled over, very bored with all the shouting. 'Anyway, so what? Who cares?' Magnificent mumbled.

Val tried to ensure Alex would not go to the Witches' Council about this mistake. She shouted at Magnificent, and he replied, 'Who cares? It's only a little old message.'

Val shouted, 'Oh, you silly old cat, it was important. You have eaten it. Now no one can find out what it was. It could have been the most important thing that has ever happened to me. It could have been the invite.'

Alex screamed once again at them both, telling them that he had just lost Gerbils and their disrespectful behaviour was not going to be tolerated. 'I am going to tell all of this to the Witches' Council.'

Magnificent just turned around, got closer to the fire, and relaxed. He found the whole situation very stressful. Anyway, it was not really his problem. I mean, how could it be his fault?

Alex wandered around looking for the remains of his friend, still very unhappy at the whole situation. And if you have ever seen a massive eagle in an angry state, you would let him complete his search.

Val asked, 'Are you finished? Is there anything I can do to help?'

'No, just help me look,' Alex shouted. 'Come on, hurry up. I am not leaving till the gerbil is found,' he told her.

Magnificent looked to see a little figure jumping around in the corner of the room, just by the door. He grabbed it.

'Well, this is great!' Gerbils shouted.

'Put Gerbils down!' Alex shouted, jumping towards Magnificent with great delight at seeing his new friend safe and well.

'That was great fun,' the wee gerbil called Gerbils told them all.

'Are you mad?' Alex asked Gerbils. 'That silly old cat nearly just ate you. That was just amazing that you survived. You, my little friend, are truly the luckiest gerbil I have ever met.'

Gerbils was still jumping around, shouting at Magnificent. 'Go on then, silly old cat, have another go. I dare you,' Gerbils tormented Magnificent. 'I am not afraid of you.'

Alex told Gerbils, this brave little message, to stop. 'Leave that cat alone before you are actually eaten.'

Magnificent stared at little Gerbils, bemused that this snack had gotten away. 'Seems you have no fear at all. But can you tell me, how did you exactly survive? This is what I would like to know.'

'Well,' Gerbils replied, 'your teeth are not the sharpest, old cat. They are nearly as sharp as the boulders in your head,' he replied once again, trying to torment Magnificent at his inability to eat him.

They were then both interrupted by Val and Alex.

'Thankfully you're alive,' they both screamed at Gerbils, for different reasons of course. Val because the Witches' Council did not take kindly to their messages being eaten, and Alex because he had never had a friend before. And of course, Magnificent cared not at all. Surely, it had nothing to do with him anyway.

Gerbils interrupted them all. 'I still have my message to deliver, so if you all don't mind, may I get on with it, please?'

Val's face lit up with excitement. 'Yes, of course.'

Alex was just happy to see his wee friend alive. 'Gerbils,' Alex shouted, 'you have to be the bravest message ever.'

Gerbils cleared his throat and began.

Dear Val, Witch,

Following your successful invention of broomsticks that fly, allowing flight for the first time for our kind, you are hereby notified that you will attend the Great Gathering, where you are entered for the Witch of the Year Award. Failure to attend will, of course, be punished.

Please attend at this address as requested: The Great Castle, Isle of Skye.

Attend on the day before 31st October this year. This message is to formally invite you to present your invention, with the possibility of winning the Witch of the Year Award. This message was delivered by Gerbils the Gerbil on behalf of the Great Witches' Council.

Now Gerbils looked up at Alex. 'Is it time for us to fly once again?' he asked, hardly able to wait. He ran towards Alex. 'Come on then, let's do this. And this time, if you don't mind, I will jump on before you take off. Is that okay with you?'

Alex smiled as he helped his new friend onto his back.

This had been one very strange delivery. Nearly eaten by a crazy old cat, and oh, that witch who was completely mad, Gerbils told Alex.

'I know,' Alex replied. 'You scared me, my friend.'

Alex could not wait to get back to the castle and tell them in the office. Oh, they were going to absolutely love this one.

Val could not wait to see her old friend Dave and tell him of her nomination for the Witch of the Year. She was in with a chance of all her dreams coming true, and it was all because of Dave. Val felt on top of the world as she thought about the friendship and love they shared.

Magnificent - The Cat

Chapter 4
On the Guest List

Val made plans to go into the Great Caledonian Forest with her ever-willing cat, Magnificent, even though his plans would, of course, never include a trip into a cold, dark place that was always wet and sometimes even snowing. He hated leaving his most happy spot in front of the warm open fire that filled his old body with a cosy glow.

'Magnificent, come on,' Val shouted. 'It's time, and we need to get the wood picked up and, of course, look in on Dave.'

Slowly, Magnificent wandered towards the old cart, dragging an old blanket with him. Val gave him a look. 'You do realise you have fur?'

He just looked up at her and told her to hurry up. 'Sooner we leave, sooner we are back.' He jumped into the cart, wrapping the blanket around himself and telling Val to get a move on.

Off they set. The old cart creaked and squeaked into action as Val pulled it along. Magnificent briefly pulled the blanket down and stuck his face out to ask Val, 'Why aren't you using that broomstick of yours?'

'You can't carry wood on a broomstick, grumpy old cat,' Val replied. He just pulled the blanket over himself and fell asleep. Slowly, she moved through the Great Caledonian Forest, collecting wood and dragging the squeaky, rickety cart with the annoying old cat snoring and farting.

Suddenly, she heard a noise in the surrounding forest. 'Magnificent, wake up. There's someone following us,' she said in a quiet voice. 'Come on, you need to wake up. I am frightened.' Val tried to get her ever-loyal cat interested.

'What is it?' Magnificent asked, giving a sigh.

Val replied, 'Someone or something is following us.'

'Really?' came the grumpy reply from this most uncaring cat.

'Why don't you help me?' Val hissed at Magnificent. 'You are always so awkward,' she told her ever-fearless, annoying cat. He, of course, just pulled his blanket up and started snoring once again.

Then came the loudest noise yet that poor Val had ever heard, followed by a thunderous shaking of the ground. 'What on earth was that?' Val thought to herself as she shook Magnificent awake.

The cat stretched and told Val to keep the noise down. He looked up at her, and she looked terrified. Puzzled by this, Magnificent asked, 'What's going on?'

She looked at him, screaming, 'I should have got a dog!'

'Well, what was it?' Magnificent asked again.

'Don't know, but at least it's stopped,' Val told him. 'Come on, let's get a move on.' They started on their way towards her old friend Dave at a faster pace.

Val and Magnificent arrived, and Dave the tree greeted them. 'It has been a while. How are you doing?'

Val replied, 'We are doing just fine,' not letting on how scared she had been.

'I hear you have finally been nominated for the Witch of the Year,' Dave told Val.

'How did you find that out?' Val said, surprised that Dave already knew.

'Well, I found out from a little fan of yours. He has been your greatest fan for many years. He has been with you every step of the way. I think that's quite a compliment,' Dave told Val.

'It's a bit, how do you say, creepy,' Val replied.

At that, once again, a massive noise shook the ground, and the trees bent.

'Well,' Dave said, 'you have just upset your biggest fan.'

'Really?' Val asked. 'I wondered just what that noise was we had heard on the way to see you today.'

'Well, just over there.' At that, the smallest leaf bug she had ever seen crawled out.

'Do I know him?' Val asked Dave, now curious about what was going on.

'Yes, do you not remember? That's him,' Dave told Val.

'What? That wee bug is making that noise?' Val was still uncertain. 'Have I met you before?' she asked, looking down at the wee bug.

'Bert the Brave, that's my name,' came a polite reply.

'What?' Val leaned over as she could barely hear.

Bert the Brave spoke up once again. 'I have tried to buy all your inventions and have followed everything you have done. I even watched as your front door locked you out, just to make sure you were okay. And remember me from when Dave flew up nearly into space?'

'Well, Brave Bert, aren't you just the sweetest thing?' came a slightly patronising reply from Val. She had, of course, forgotten but did not wish to upset Bert.

Bert the Brave stopped her to correct her. 'It's Bert the Brave, that's my name.'

'Well, that's nice. Now you take care of yourself,' Val told the wee bug.

'He would like to go with you,' Dave told Val.

Bert - The Brave

'Where?' Val asked.

'To the Great Gathering, of course,' Dave replied. 'You would make your greatest fan's dreams come true.'

'I am not taking a bug on holiday. There'll be plenty of them in the castle, I am sure,' Val replied.

'Oh well, I did tell him I would ask, so if that's the way you feel, I will not ask again. However, it's only fair you tell your number one fan he's not welcome. And, by the way, I was going to tell you something interesting that I have found out about my small branches.'

Val was not bothered one way or the other about Bert, not really. He was so small he would not have taken up any space at all. But Dave telling her something new about him—that was always worth finding out.

'Okay,' Val said, looking down at Bert. 'You can come. One question for you, little one—how and why do you make that noise?'

'When I am happy, mostly, and if I am really scared.'

A big mistake was about to happen once Val asked if Bert was happy. 'Oh yes,' he replied, and he made that massive noise. Dave then asked him to be just a wee bit quieter. Excitedly, Bert replied, 'Okay, I am just off to get packed.'

Magnificent had gone. He did this now and again. Bert the Brave was already in the cart, and Val was saying her goodbyes to her old friend Dave. Val also collected, as agreed a long time ago, the fallen branches that would make the next batch of flying broomsticks.

While parting, she asked him curiously what this new thing was that he had discovered about himself.

'We will speak once you return from the Great Gathering. Well, goodbye for now, and thanks for everything you have done for me.'

She then hugged the biggest part of Dave and gave him a tender kiss.

With the wood collected, Val started the journey home. The cart was full and heavy, and the light was fading.

Bert the Brave spoke, 'We are nearly home, and tomorrow is going to be a big day in my life. Are we going to fly there? How long will it take? I will, of course, be bringing my Last Will and Testament up to date.'

Val now clearly remembered Bert the Brave. She also thought of Magnificent and the law firms, which seemed to be springing up everywhere. She recalled heading to space and the little leaf bug who had been with them on that day.

Bert the Brave now asked lots and lots of questions, far too many for Val to answer all at once, and she was struggling with the heavy cart. Bert the Brave was so inquisitive. To be honest, it was a refreshing change from Magnificent in comparison. But she did miss the silence of that grumpy old cat.

They were now approaching the edge of the village, which was a welcome sight.

They were home. Magnificent, of course, was lying by the open fire in his most cosy spot, awaiting them.

'How did you get back so quickly?' Val asked her furry friend.

'Well,' Magnificent replied, 'I am a cat with a much better sense of direction than you. I did watch you two for a wee while, but you took so long. Anyway, food ready, fire on, and of course, I am just splendid.'

He, to be fair, did have a habit of ensuring he was well taken care of.

Bert the Brave asked, 'Where will I be sleeping?'

'You can sleep anywhere you like,' Val told her newfound best friend.

'Great,' said Bert the Brave, now imagining waking up in Val's bed next to her. 'Where is your room?' he asked.

'No, not a chance. You are not sleeping in my room at all, do you understand, Bert the Brave?'

The leaf bug was so happy that Val had remembered his name, and, well, just because of the general excitement, he let out his noise, which of course woke up the entire village and shook everything in it.

He then ran at Val to give her a hug. She tried to run but fell over Magnificent, and he then ran into the wall. Bert the Brave once again let out that loud noise, this time because he was sad that he had upset everyone.

'Stop, please stop,' Val cried out. The village dogs, cats, and any other creatures were now all wide awake. Widespread panic engulfed the entire village as everything had been shaken and, oh, that noise. It took hours before it all started to return to normal.

'Well, sorry about that,' Bert the Brave told them all as the whole village, Magnificent, and Val tried to settle down. Bert the Brave found a small, quiet spot next to Magnificent, and then they all went to bed, thinking of the Great Gathering and the castle.

Chapter 5

Happy Castle Landings

Next morning, Val woke up excited. This was her chance to fly into history, and of course she thought she had a great chance to win the Witch of the Year, but now, because of Bert the Brave, all must remain calm.

Bert the Brave was, of course, up and wide awake. No one knew where he was, as he had decided to explore the house. Magnificent was up, making food, and asked in a very quiet voice,

'Val, is the wee bug staying long?'

Val quietly replied, 'Not certain.'

'What have you packed for the Castle?' asked Val.

'Well,' replied Magnificent, 'all the stuff over there.' The cat pointed to a mountain of items, including the contents of his entire wardrobe, a sink of logs in case he needed to build a fire, a bed, and of course four suitcases, the contents of which Magnificent was unwilling to reveal.

'What's this?' Val asked, trying not to shout. 'You cannot take all that!' in the softest voice possible. 'Your bed, your wardrobe... have you lost the plot?'

'I guess that you will be taking everything you need?' Magnificent replied.

'Yes, that is precisely what I will be doing,' said Val.

'So will I,' Magnificent said, sticking his tail in the air and prancing away, waving it proudly.

'No, you will not,' Val told Magnificent, trying to get the last word in. 'We are going by broomstick, so get it sorted out. Anyway, what would a cat need all that stuff for?'

'Well, you never can tell,' replied Magnificent, glancing back at Val to give that snooty look he had perfected over many years.

Val was now very annoyed at having to argue with Magnificent, but she could not shout at this most annoying cat. She quietly negotiated with him, trying to ensure that everything would fit onto a broomstick.

'I will get you a new soft bed to put in your favourite spot beside the fire if you go minimalistic,' Val offered.

Magnificent looked at Val and asked, 'Does that mean I am taking nothing?'

'Well,' came the reply, 'not nothing, but a lot less than you are taking just now.'

'Okay, a new soft bed to go into my favourite place it is then.' Magnificent, the master negotiator, started to put everything away. Val realised that this was the cat's plan all along. If there is one thing we all know about this cat, it is that the most valuable thing to him was that cosy spot beside the fire. Magnificent welcomed this most unexpected surprise.

'Right, let's get food,' Val told Magnificent, 'and of course Rodney, the broomstick, ready.' He liked to be told where he was going a few hours before they left.

'Are there any more broomsticks we could take?' Val asked, thinking that they would make good presents for the Witches Council.

'Maybe two more,' Magnificent replied, heading out to check. Finally, this stubborn cat was doing something he had been asked to do by Val.

'Okay, I will get them ready,' Magnificent told Val.

'Rodney, you awake?'

'Yes, that I am. Where are we going tonight?'

'The castle, no less,' replied Magnificent.

'Superb, how many are we taking?'

'Tree bug called Bert the Brave, me, and of course Val. Plus luggage.'

'How much luggage?' Rodney, the broomstick, was now mentally preparing, pacing up and down to make himself ready.

'Thanks for letting me know,' Rodney told Magnificent as he headed back into the house. Magnificent was now returning to his favourite spot beside the fire, making himself cosy and dreaming of just how soft his new bed would be. As he fell deeper into sleep, the snoring and loud farting began. Val opened the window to vent the smell, looking at her furry friend with disgust. All needed to get some sleep before the journey.

Val slept for a little while before nightfall. It was time for them all to fly towards the castle.

Bert the Brave jumped on Rodney, beside himself with excitement. Magnificent slumped onto the back, and Val sat in the middle. Everything they needed, including the two new broomsticks, was packed.

'Rodney, you ready?' Val asked.

'Yes, but I will give a wee safety briefing if you wish to,' Rodney replied.

'Please hang on tight, this is your safety announcement,' Val told him.

At that, they were off, flying towards the Isle of Skye and the castle. The moon shone bright, guiding their way. The journey itself should take only about an hour if everything went to plan.

Val asked if everyone was okay and praised Rodney for flying so well. Bert the Brave once again thanked Val for letting him come along. Val's only words were to tell Bert the Brave that there was no need to thank them; it was their pleasure.

Upon hearing those kind words, this most sensitive little one let out a scream. Val managed to persuade Bert the Brave not to do this. However, the inevitable was about to happen.

Bert the Brave let out a scream, upset that he had upset Val. Rodney, shocked at the scream, headed straight for the sea over which they were travelling. The speed at which they were approaching the water was truly terrifying. Nonetheless, that was where they were heading, faster and faster.

'Rodney, pull up! Pull up, Rodney, please pull up!' Val screamed.

This made Bert the Brave scream even more, and everything they were trying to do seemed too late. They hit the water at about 80mph, creating a massive splash.

'Really?' Val screamed. 'Really, the most important journey we have ever taken, and you have done this.'

'It's not my fault,' Rodney said. 'That—Bert, why on earth would he scream?'

Magnificent, not best pleased that he had been woken from his lovely sleep, shouted, 'Has anyone seen Bert? Val, you seen Bert. Come on, where is the little bug? Has anyone seen him?'

They looked around at the water. All were floating, unable to see very much, to be honest. They all started calling out for Bert the Brave, screaming, 'Come on now, Bert the Brave, where are you? Speak up, Bert, where are you?'

Bert the Brave was gone. Magnificent was now frantic. He had started to like the little fellow and did not want to see any harm come to him. Everyone seemed to forget that they were in the sea.

Rodney, the broomstick, decided it was time for him to exit the water. He gave himself a shake and then hovered just above Val. Magnificent jumped back on top of the broomstick. Their luggage and the other broomsticks remained strapped to Rodney.

'Shall we look for him?' asked Magnificent.

'Yes,' Val replied. 'Let's look for him. He can't be far.'

Rodney circled the area in the hope of spotting Bert the Brave. In the distance, they saw a small island—well, more of a rock, really. They headed towards it, thinking that the leaf bug might have made it onto it.

'Prepare to land!' the words were shouted. Rodney executed this with his usual finesse, and they smashed straight into the rock.

'Another fine landing, Rodney, well done,' Val said, shaking herself off.

Then, to everyone's surprise, the small rock spoke. 'What do you lot think you are doing?' it asked. 'Why have you landed on me? I have feelings, you know. I really do have feelings. You lot walking all over me is not very pleasant.'

'So sorry,' Val said, trying to apologise while explaining that they were looking for a little bug. 'Maybe you have seen him?'

'No,' the rock replied, 'but I did see a little thing called Bert the Brave. Is it possible this is what you are all looking for?'

'That's great,' they all shouted. 'Just great. Where has he gone?'

'Flew off that direction, towards the big castle,' the rock told them. 'He couldn't stand what he had done to you all. Reckoned that you would all be better off without him, so he's going back to the castle. Anyway, when are you all going to get off me? You are really starting to annoy me.'

Rodney asked the rock if they could have a few moments just to get a little bit drier.

'Well, can you hurry up?' the rock replied. 'You all aren't in any danger, are you?'

'No,' came the reply.

Magnificent climbed on Rodney. Val took a few moments to look towards the castle, thinking just how beautiful it looked in the moonlight.

'Hurry up,' Rodney said. 'We need to get off this rock.'

Magnificent shouted that he was already on, so hurry up. Rodney then took off immediately, heading towards the castle. One small problem—they had left Val behind.

Val stared into the darkness, looking towards the castle. 'Just great. Why have they left me? Can this get any worse?' Val was now alone on a small rock in the middle of nowhere.

'What just happened?' the rock asked Val. 'Why have they just left you on me?'

'I have not a clue,' replied Val.

At the castle, Rodney and Magnificent flew around, looking for Bert the Brave. They did not see him. Magnificent asked Rodney to land at the castle. Magnificent was at the very front, staring out to see any trace of Bert the Brave. 'Hurry up and find a landing spot,' was then spoken by Magnificent. This was without doubt one of the silliest things possible to say to Rodney.

Rodney was now in full "get it done" mode and spotted a landing place close to a large wall, beside some greenhouses next to power lines.

'Right, time to land, hang on,' were the last words spoken as Rodney dived down towards this most unsuitable spot. The power lines caught the end of the broomstick, and every couple of seconds Magnificent would light up.

Then they spun around, slamming into the large wall, which was the main wall of the castle. Rodney pulled up, pulling the power lines ever tighter around Magnificent. He now resembled a cartoon character from something just blown up. Fur was sticking up everywhere and the noise was unbelievable.

'Don't worry,' Rodney called out. 'I am going in again.'

This time, the greenhouse was demolished by the final attempt at landing, which Rodney was pleased to report was complete, proudly letting poor old Magnificent know he was free to disembark.

Magnificent ran from the utter devastation that Rodney had caused, pleased to now be on the land. He looked towards the broomsticks, and in fairness, Rodney, sensing that Magnificent was unhappy, tried not to make eye contact.

'Sorry about that,' came an apology from Rodney. 'I couldn't see anything, to be honest. The spray from the sea has gotten in my eyes.'

Magnificent, shaken and most certainly stirred, started to look for Bert the Brave, trying to pull together some dignity after this most horrible experience.

'I can't see him around here,' repeated Rodney. 'Cannot see Val either. Wonder where they have all gone.'

Rodney, now realising Val too was missing, asked Magnificent, 'I think we might have dropped Val off somewhere?' He then started to think.

'We did pick up Val, didn't we?' Both now realised that maybe they had not.

'Oh, I fear that we may not have done,' Rodney said. 'She's not going to be happy about this,' said Magnificent.

Back on the rock, Val was pacing up and down, looking into the night sky and wondering which one of the two of them she was going to deal with first. Rodney could be made into firewood, and that cat could be a nice stew. Yes, it would be a Magnificent stew.

Suddenly, the rock spoke up. 'When are you planning to be leaving?' asked the rock, becoming increasingly annoyed at having been crashed into, and now the very thing that had crashed into her would not leave.

'I, Val Witch, do not need you giving me any hassle,' came an angry reply.

'Well, only asking,' came the reply from the rock. 'By the way, I am just about to dive to the bottom of the sea, so if you are hanging on, hopefully you will still be there once we come back up. Good luck, and by the way, my name is Shawna.'

At that, down they went. To say that Val was surprised would be an understatement. Nevertheless, down in the middle of the sea they were. Floating around in the darkness was not what Val had expected. Now she was afraid of drowning. Val was also afraid that if she did not turn up by nine o'clock as promised, there would be trouble. But mostly, she was afraid of drowning.

Shawna swam around, calling out her beautiful sounds. The noise was simply beautiful. Val spoke to Shawna.

'Shawna, how is it possible that I can breathe under the water? We must be fifteen to twenty metres down in the sea. It should not be possible. I should have drowned by now.'

'You are under my protection and so I cannot let you down. I wish there were more like you,' Shawna reassured Val, still noticing her annoyance at both Rodney and Magnificent flying off and forgetting her.

'Shawna,' Val said, 'it might have just been a simple mistake.' Val was enchanted by this experience. It was as if Shawna had created a massive bubble of air that Val could use to breathe.

Meanwhile, back at the castle—well, more precisely outside the castle—Rodney and Magnificent were trying to organise themselves.

'Right, Rodney,' Magnificent said. 'You go to where we were the last time, where the rock was, and look for Val.'

'Okay,' Rodney replied. 'I am right on it.' Off Rodney went, flying into the night skies.

How am I going to find them all? Magnificent thought. *And it's now nearly six o'clock. If Val has not made it by nine, the Witches Council will not be happy.*

'Bert the Brave, where would he have gone?' Magnificent thought. *It's a mess,* he said out loud. 'Just a big mess. We need help.'

At that, Magnificent saw a sign advertising Eagle Investigations: *"All work undertaken with a professional touch."* Off Magnificent headed to the offices. He went inside. *"Eagle Couriers"* was written above the door leading inside. Magnificent wandered through and up the stairs. Then, in front of him, was the office he needed.

'Come in!' a voice from within called out. 'Hurry up now. You can sit just there. I have been expecting you. Please sit down and tell me how we can help. You have lost someone? What a shame, this is always a shame. I hate when that happens.' She never even stopped to breathe.

'Anyway,' she continued, 'we need to find Val the Witch quickly, and sooner rather than later.'

'But how did you find this out?' Magnificent asked.

'Well, that's an easy one. Everyone watched you lot land. It's the funniest thing we have ever seen. You are no eagles, that's for sure. Anyway, my name is Elisabeth. It's my company and I will be assigning you a case worker.'

At that, she screamed, 'Colin, get in! Need to speak to you.'

Colin ran in, very flustered with all the preparations for the Great Gathering and now this. 'What is it?' he asked, annoyed at yet more to do.

'This is Magnificent,' Elisabeth told Colin, turning to point at him. 'He has lost Val the Witch somewhere out there,' pointing to the sea, 'and I wish you to get it sorted out. Colin, there is no time to waste, so please act as quickly as you can.'

Colin ran out towards the eagles and told them all to take to the skies without delay. They, of course, did. Elisabeth then turned to Magnificent. 'Well, now this means you will pay me, as you, my fine friend, have just engaged the services of Eagle Investigations.'

'Yes, of course,' he replied. 'Once you find and bring back Val, nothing until then,' Magnificent told Elisabeth.

'And what about Bert the Brave?' he asked. Elisabeth smiled and said, 'You have no need to look for Bert the Brave, believe me.' Magnificent tried to say something else but was now being asked to leave.

Meanwhile, Val and her new friend Shawna were travelling. Val had no clue where or how long it would take to get back. The eagles were, of course, doing as they had been told and looking for Val, as was Rodney, and still no one had found Bert the Brave or Val. Worse still, it was nearly nine o'clock, and the Witches Council did not accept excuses.

Magnificent continued to look for Bert the Brave. He was heading towards yet more stairs and walkways of this enormous castle and was really worried about the little leaf bug and, of course, Val. He started to think that this search was going to be fruitless but had no plans to give up, hoping that Rodney would have more luck. Maybe even the eagles would find Val. He missed her so much.

Rodney was now starting to head back to the castle, having failed to find anything. He had to avoid the eagles but then spotted a small figure in a window in the castle. *Could that be a leaf bug?* he thought. Rodney flew closer and closer, eventually flying straight into the window. Bert the Brave tried to jump out of the way, and Rodney completed his mission as Bert the Brave was now on the broomstick, heading out of the castle.

Rodney then flew down to find Magnificent. 'Well, you will never guess what I have found.'

Magnificent, in no mood for this, shouted, 'What now?'

At that moment, a little leaf bug that answered to the name Bert the Brave popped up.

'Oh, thank goodness you are okay. You have had us all so worried,' Bert the Brave told them. He was so sorry and then started to cry.

'Now stop that!' both Rodney and Magnificent pleaded. 'We have things to do. Remember, we have still not found Val.'

Bert the Brave looked like he was going to do that thing again. Everyone was covering their ears. Then the inevitable happened. The ground shook, sending a massive shock wave out to sea.

Bert the Brave then stopped. 'So sorry, it's okay. I will be fine now.'

All looked terrified, apart from Bert the Brave. He just turned and told them, 'I am fine now.' No one said a thing.

Magnificent turned to everyone, looked at them, and said, 'I wish to hear nothing of this at all. Let's try and get through this night without anything else going wrong. Do you all understand? Rodney, are you listening to me?'

'Yes, okay, I understand.'

'Bert the Brave, you are okay?'

'Yes,' came the reply.

'Okay then, no point in us all bringing this up again.'

Colin then showed up. 'What on earth are you lot doing? Have you seen the state of the poor fishing fleet? They've been pushed up onto the beach. There was a massive noise, then that wave that hit. Do you lot know anything about this?'

'Well, Colin,' Magnificent said, 'it's maybe best if we discuss this over there, away from Rodney and, of course, Bert the Brave.' Magnificent quietly explained about Bert the Brave and how, if upset, he could get, shall we say, a bit tense. Colin turned to look at Rodney and Bert the Brave.

'Stop looking at him. He gets very easily upset, and we wouldn't wish to do that.' Colin walked off, telling Magnificent, 'You clearly have not one single clue about anything at all. I only came to tell you we have not found Val Witch. I must inform you that if she is not found soon, the Witches Council will, of course, order she be found and detained to await trial.'

Magnificent turned to reassure Bert the Brave. 'You are fine. We will sort all this out somehow,' he told the now broken-hearted leaf bug. 'We will find Val, and all will turn out well.' Not certain just how all this was going to sort itself out, but better to be optimistic than to believe that they would never see Val again.

Shawna was still travelling effortlessly through the sea. Val was fighting back tears, telling Shawna that if she did not get to the castle, the Witches Council would order her death. She also said that she missed her cat, Magnificent.

Shawna told her to pull herself together; she had no time to go back. She was a world traveller and had no time whatsoever.

It was nine o'clock. Colin went back to tell Magnificent that he would have to inform the Witches Council of the situation.

'Well, time's up, old chap. Sorry about this, but the eagles have been sent a message that this was not a "Find to Represent" situation; it was a "Hunt".'

Elisabeth was standing next to him. 'So sorry, Magnificent, but I will have to tell the eagles—Alex, Sandy, and Ian—that they must bring Val straight to the castle jail. Of course, the good news is that the

Great Witches Council will now be paying for the recovery of Val. She will not escape us.'

Colin then told Rodney and Magnificent that they must go home. He did not tell Bert the Brave. 'Please don't take this personally, but you all have no reason to be here and must leave. Of course, you will be informed of any developments.' He turned to wave them a cheerful goodbye.

Elisabeth headed towards the Great Witches Council; they would already know precisely what was going on and were deep in debate about what to do next.

Pam spoke to the wise old Owl, Tweet. 'I think I know what's happened.'

'What?' Tweet asked.

'She has decided the pressure was too much and has run away, leaving us with her crazy friends.'

Tweet pulled her glasses down and stared at her. 'Shut up, please. That was most unhelpful.'

Tweet then turned to Elisabeth. 'The eagles—Alex, Sandy, and Ian—they have been to her last location?'

'Yes, they have,' Elisabeth replied.

'And they see nothing?'

'Correct. They have been there for nearly an hour. Rodney, the broomstick, has also searched, so we know she is not there.'

'Well, that being the case, we should conclude that she is missing.'

They all cheered, amazed at Tweet's remarkable ability to find the truth.

Rodney, Magnificent, and, of course, Bert the Brave were coming up with a plan.

'Right, let's get on, Rodney, and have a look where Val was last seen.'

'Yes, let's go.'

Shawna was ready to dive once again. Val asked her, 'How far away are we from the castle?'

'Oh, about thirty miles, that's all.'

One dive and she had gone thirty miles. *If she dives once again, I will be sixty miles away from the castle,* thought Val. *Maybe I could swim.*

'Shawna, can you let me off here?' Val asked.

Shawna was shocked at this and told her that without her, she could die out in the sea.

'Shawna, if I don't get back to the castle, that's going to happen anyway.'

'If you have a boat, that would help,' Val joked. But much to Val's surprise, came a most unexpected reply: yes, Shawna had a boat, and if Val wished, that would be no problem at all.

'Yeah, a boat to get back—that would be great, Shawna.'

'Yeah, like I said, you are more than welcome to it if you wish. I even think that there might be a crew on it still.'

Val thought this could be a trick. But she said, 'Ah, yes, that would be very kind of you.'

Val lingered at the front beside Shawna's mouth, waiting for the boat to appear, not certain just where it would come from. Maybe Shawna had some way of contacting passing ships and boats.

Shawna then explained, 'It will not so much pop out... more like poop out. Yours, at the wrong end.'

'Well,' Val asked, 'just how did it get there?'

Shawna explained that she always liked to help anything in trouble and would simply swallow things that looked like they were in trouble, keeping them safe from harm or just in case they could be used.

'How long have you had the boat?' Val asked inquisitively.

'Not sure, forgot it was in there.'

'To be honest,' came the answer from Shawna, 'but you are welcome to use it.'

Val gave Shawna a strange look.

'Well, I am very old. Cannot be expected to remember everything. Anyway, they will all get home now,' Shawna replied.

A few minutes later, and as promised, out came a boat, fully equipped. The three crew members rubbed their eyes, all of them with long beards. They looked at Val standing on the whale, Shawna, and shouted, 'Hurry up. Get off quickly, she will eat you!'

Val gently thanked Shawna for her help and asked her if she was happy to let them all go.

'But of course. I only ever try to save things from the sea and oceans that look to need help.'

'I understand,' Val told Shawna, most grateful, as were her newfound friends. 'I do, however, admittedly find it difficult to let them go once I have rescued them.'

'Perhaps,' Shawna told Val, 'I need to work this out. Maybe it's time I had a good clean out. I hope you let us all get far away before you do this.'

Val laughed.

Val and her newfound friends now decided that, upon hearing this, a little more urgency to swiftly vacate the situation was needed. She stepped from the whale onto the boat, thanked the beautiful whale, and watched as the kind giant left them. Shawna was truly a kind whale, just a little misunderstood; she would rescue anything in distress, Val told the sailors.

The sailors, named Captain Billy Low, Moose, and, of course, Donald, were on their boat, the Stratheliott, twenty years ago when their dog, Brogan, took a dislike to a red-coloured sailing ship. She created a massive fight on the boat as Captain Billy Low tried to bring the dog under control, but he was nipped by the dog, causing him to fall down the stairs.

The boat would at this point be heading, much to Brogan's delight, towards the sailing ship with the red sail, with no one steering it. They would nearly hit the sailing ship. Off into the distance the sailing ship went, but the boat, known as the Stratheliott, was caught by a massive wave as Captain Billy and his crew tried to get up to the wheelhouse. The boat was thrown into the air and lost all ability to steer or remain seaworthy. It was presumed that all the crew, including Brogan the dog, had been lost at sea.

The truth was that Shawna had swallowed the boat whole to rescue both the boat and its crew. They had remained in the belly of the whale for twenty years.

Apparently, they had all learned how to play musical instruments and had made their boat seaworthy once again. Val was stunned when she heard this story. 'You are all so brave. What about Brogan the dog?'

At that, a collie named Brogan walked slowly towards Val in the hope of being petted.

'And are you lot any good with these musical instruments?'

At that, they all started to play, and Val had to admit they were good.

'We plan to call our band Captain Billy and the Fisherman. What do you think?' they asked.

'Great,' Val replied. 'Sound and look amazing.'

'Anyway, lass, what about you? How can we help?' Captain Billy asked.

'Well, if you can get me to the Castle Isle of Sky as soon as you can, that would be great.'

Two hours later, they approached the coastline next to the castle and asked Val if this was close enough. Val smiled and said, 'This is just great. Captain Billy and your crew... twenty years away, travelling the world in Shawna the whale.'

They let Val off at the castle and stood on dry land, unsure of just what to do next. Then they saw a rugby team on the beach. They were called over to join in, taking musical instruments with them. It looked like the first ever recorded beach party.

Val looked up at the castle. How was she going to fix this, she wondered? The problem was it was now half past eleven, and she knew that the Witches Council would almost certainly be looking for her.

Her chances of winning Witch of the Year were slipping away. They would almost certainly have decided that she was now guilty of failing to be on time. Not turning up to an order made by the Witches Council was a very bad thing to do.

Then she heard the wonderful sound of Magnificent and Rodney.

'Look, it's Val down there!' Rodney and Magnificent flew down to pick her up. Naturally, they smashed into the ground beside her.

'Great landing. You are getting a wee bit better, Rodney,' Val said, remembering that the way to get the best from Rodney was with encouragement.

'You all okay?' Val asked, looking at them scattered along the beach.

Rodney shook himself. 'That was better,' he shouted. 'Getting really close to the perfect landing, I think.'

Magnificent was in a tree close by. He jumped down and rubbed himself as close as he could against Val, purring continuously with contentment that she was back.

Bert the Brave then appeared, flying down from the top of the castle ramparts. He grabbed hold of Val's leg and told her he was so sorry about his wee problem. Val reassured him.

'Right, come on, we need to fix this,' said Val. 'And just where did you get to, Bert the Brave? All of us were scared that we were not going to see you again. We need to speak about that. Running off is never good; we should always try and solve what's gone wrong. But I am so happy we are altogether now.'

'We could ask you the same,' they all shouted at her. 'Just what happened?'

'Look,' Val told them, 'we must solve this first. I will tell you what happened later. Let's figure out what room we were meant to be in, get in it, and make out that I was there all the time. Okay, now the castle is up there, we are down here... just how do we do this?'

'We have Rodney,' Magnificent told Val. 'He could simply fly you up to it.'

'But we still need to get in,' Val replied.

'Bert the Brave could get in. What do you say, Bert the Brave? You up for that?' Magnificent asked.

'Of course, I can do this,' came the excited reply. They all braced themselves, waiting on Bert to do his thing. But surprisingly, he didn't hesitate. Bert the Brave climbed up the side of the castle and got inside.

Colin was in there, doing his role as the administrator. He was sitting at the end of the corridor where all the guests would be living. Bert the Brave strolled past him and went underneath the doors, searching each room. Some of the things he saw were best not spoken about, but then he found the room Val should have been in. He went to the window and threw down an ornament. He waited a couple of seconds and then shouted to Magnificent standing below.

Magnificent looked up and was hit straight on the head with the ornament. The poor cat was now dazed and wondering what had just happened. *Just what was that?* he thought, as he lay on his back mumbling strange words like, 'Mummy, the lights are twinkling... Rock on, baby, let's all rock on.'

A few moments later, Magnificent was back with them all. He was not best pleased but tried to remain both calm and composed, only because if he did not, Bert the Brave would do that thing again, which would benefit no one.

'Right, Rodney...' Val was about to say something but was interrupted.

'Eagles! Look out!' Alex, Sandy, and Ian were returning from looking for Val, and as we all know, eagles spot everything. They miss nothing.

They all hid apart from Bert the Brave. He threw another ornament down, hitting poor old Magnificent again. Val looked over at her friend. The eagles passed overhead, and Magnificent was walking about once again, dazed from being hit on the head twice more by two heavy ornaments.

'That wee...!' Magnificent started to shout, but Val gave him a big cuddle, trying to comfort her old furry friend. She held him gently as Magnificent slowly got back to his normal self. He gave her a very angry look before they started to work out what to do next.

Val called to Rodney. 'Right. Get me up there without crashing. Can you do that?'

'I'll give it my best try.'

Up into the air they went on Rodney the broomstick until they were directly opposite the window leading to the room. Rodney then got ready for the final approach and flew towards the window. Straight into the room—the perfect approach, apart from the speed.

They hit the far wall at about thirty miles per hour. Val was thrown backwards onto the bed. Bert the Brave did his thing, the entire castle shook, and alarms were set off everywhere. Chaos. Complete and utter chaos.

'Rodney, get him out of here!' Val shouted.

Bert the Brave got on Rodney. They left the room. Val jumped into bed.

Magnificent was still dazed down below from Bert the Brave's handy work.

Colin was running up and down to each room.

'Hurry!' he yelled into each room. 'Head to the main hall!'

The room doors all banged open, and a mad stampede towards the main hall took place.

Val ran towards the main hall. Tweet the Owl awaited there, screaming out orders and telling Colin to count that everyone was okay.

'Hurry up, Colin!' Tweet shouted.

'One extra. I cannot explain it, but there is one too many,' Colin shouted, deeply upset at this horrible outcome.

'What are you saying?' Tweet shouted. 'Count them again.'

Colin counted once more, and still there was one extra.

'Tweet, there is one extra. I cannot explain this... Wait,' Colin then said, 'is that Val the Witch?'

Val did her best to look surprised.

'Yes, it is,' she said.

'Tweet, we have found Val Witch!' Colin shouted above the noise. 'Look, it really is the missing Witch Val.'

Tweet the Owl then turned to look directly at Val. 'Just where have you been?' he asked.

'I was sleeping in the room after my long journey and then heard a loud noise. Is everything okay?' Val replied.

Tweet was not best pleased.

'Colin, if you were not such an asset to this organisation, I would fire you in the big fire. Now, let's get everyone back to their rooms.'

'And might I take this opportunity to apologise for the disturbance,' Tweet the Owl told the castle guests as they made their way back to their rooms.

Tweet then stopped Val.

'Val, do you realise that we have all been searching for you?' he asked.

'No, I didn't. And do you know where my guests have gone? Have they arrived yet?' Val asked.

Tweet looked at her and said, 'We sent them away, thinking that you had run away or had not turned up.'

'Oh dear, that's not good,' Val replied, trying to look surprised. She then asked if it was possible to have them found.

Tweet turned to Colin and demanded that this be done with the utmost speed.

Then in came Elisabeth.

'I expect you are looking for them?' she asked as Rodney and Magnificent appeared from behind her.

'Yes,' Tweet said. 'We are.'

'Well, the bill will be on your desk in the morning, and I am happy everything has worked out. Val, might I have a word?'

Elisabeth and Val walked towards Val's room. In the politest way possible, Elisabeth explained that she knew everything and that her bill was on the way, which should be paid—or else.

A nice bit of work for Elisabeth. She had managed to get both Val and Tweet to pay for this most busy night's work. Poor Colin was still confused but was none the wiser to the night's events.

End of chapter 5

Chapter 6
Preparations Begin

The day after the night before was, by all accounts, very boring. They spent the time eating and looking around the castle. As Val turned a corner, there before her stood Alex the eagle.

'Well, would you ever,' Alex said. 'You showed up. We all hoped you were still out there so I could make more money looking for you. And how are you?'

'Just fine,' Val replied.

'And that cat of yours. I take it he is still fine?' Alex asked.

'He is,' Val politely answered. 'And Gerbils the gerbil. How's your friend doing?'

'Okay,' replied Alex, explaining that Gerbils was off delivering messages. 'I am sure he will be glad to know you are all here. Anyway, glad to see you. Enjoy your stay and I hope you win tonight.'

Well, Val thought, that was nice. She headed to the offices in the great castle. Opening the door, she was greeted by Elisabeth.

'Hi, you. How are you doing today? That was some day yesterday. Bert the Brave, he is a wee character. Is he not?'

'He is that,' Val said.

'Where did he come from, do you know?' Elisabeth asked Val.

'Not really,' Val explained. 'First met him a while back on a tree. But why are you asking?'

'No reason, just curious,' Elisabeth replied, smiling at Val. You always knew there was something else going on when you spoke to Elisabeth. What that was was never clear, but this clever witch always seemed to remain one step ahead of everyone.

Val asked, 'How much is my bill going to be?'

'Well,' Elisabeth told Val, 'if you find out anything about Bert the Brave and promise to tell me... nothing.'

'And if I find out nothing, how much?' Val asked, cautious of making a deal that might have unexpected consequences.

'Well, let's say it's in your own best interest to. Shall we just leave it at that?' Elisabeth brought the encounter to a close. 'We will speak soon, I am sure of this, so bye for now.'

Val could not help but wonder what all that was about, but she had no time just now to find out. It was time to get a new dress. She walked into the boutique. The sign above the door read: *All your clothing desires fulfilled in one place.*

'Can I help you?' came a small voice from behind the counter.

'Yes, you can,' Val said. 'I would like...'

But she was not given time to speak, as a team of enthusiastic assistants gathered around her.

'Black or grey, white or black, green or blue, maybe yellow, how about tartan? It's very popular now. Maybe we could do a combination, that would look fantastic. Have you been nominated? Are you a star witch?'

She tried to speak, but it was too late. They had already started making her clothes for tonight's Gathering.

'Please just trust us. We will create for you.'

And with that, she was hurried out of the boutique and into the street, followed by her very own assistant.

'Who are you?' Val asked the frog now following her about.

'Ashley. Been sent by Tweet. I have been told to watch you today and give you every assistance.'

'Sounds good to me,' Val replied. 'Where do you get your hair done, Ashley?'

'Nowhere at all. I have none,' Ashley replied. 'Have you not noticed I am a frog?'

'Yes,' Val answered. 'I was more asking for me. Might I ask you, where would I get my hair done?'

'Oh, I see what you mean. Just follow me.' Ashley now fully understood what Val was asking.

Two doors further down the street, they stopped in front of Mathew's Hair Emporium. Ashley and Val went in. A bear – a very large bear – greeted them.

'Sit,' said the bear. 'Sorry, not you, Ashley. You may wait over there. I fear I can do nothing with your hair, as you, my dear, have none. Now you hop off to the waiting room.

'Let's see what we can do with this hair of yours,' Mathew said, rubbing at Val's hair. 'It needs washed, blow-dried, I think, and a little off the bottom. This okay, Val, or would you like me just to create something?'

'Yeah, that sounds great. Not too much off the bottom, please.'

Val had never let anyone touch her hair before, but sometimes you just had to go with the flow. Mathew the bear was now in full creative mode.

Meanwhile, back at the castle, Magnificent was cleaning up the room after Rodney had flown into everything and Bert the Brave had done his thing. It took a few hours. Then Magnificent decided he would look over this castle.

He got as far as the biggest fireplace he had ever seen and could not resist pulling over a cushion and having a little nap. He was installed as though he had always lived there.

Construction crews were working all over the great hall in preparation for tonight. A large stage with lights had been set up, and it looked amazing. The great hall had never looked so good. This night was going to be the best ever seen. Colin was running everywhere, ensuring nothing could go wrong.

Back at the hairdresser's, Val was having her hair finished. Her long hair was looking stunning. Mathew was indeed a fantastic choice.

'Right,' said the massive bear. 'You, my dear, are ready. I have created my best work, and the good news for you is that it is on your head. You, my dear witch, look just amazing. Ashley!' Mathew shouted. 'Come and look at this!'

Ashley burst into tears. 'Val,' she said, looking at her, 'you are so beautiful.'

Val looked at the big mirror in front of her, and in fairness, she was stunning.

'Right,' Val asked Mathew, 'how much must I pay you?'

Ashley told her not to worry about it. 'It's all been taken care of. We really need to get back to the boutique.'

At the boutique, they had finished her dress, which was black with tartan trimmings. It was truly beautiful.

'We will deliver it to your room. The castle has decided they will pay for this because of all the problems last night. Is this okay?'

Val replied, 'Well, are you sure?'

'Yes, no problem. Was Ashley some help to you? Please try this on now, just to ensure it fits you well. Also, we have taken the liberty of making a small bow tie for Magnificent.'

Magnificent in a bow tie, Val thought. Now that was going to take some doing, to get the old fur ball to put that on.

Val changed into the dress. She loved it, and it fitted like nothing she had ever had before.

'The dress will be in your room in about one hour,' Ashley told her. 'You look just fantastic.'

'Why, thank you kindly,' Val replied, blushing. 'You're also looking just fantastic too.'

'Honestly?' said Ashley. 'I do?' No one had ever been so kind to her before, and it made this little frog so happy.

'Yes, that you do,' said Val, looking straight at her and repeating it. Ashley seemed to have a little sparkle of her own now.

'Well, let's get back to the room.' Val could not wait to see Magnificent and show off the dress and her amazing hair. She also needed to check if the old cat had had a bath. He was never very big on water, and she feared that Magnificent might not have realised that sea water would turn most of his fur white because of the salt. And in all honesty, he was a bit, how do you put this politely, smelly.

He was nowhere to be seen. Damn it, she thought. Where would he be? She asked Colin as he was running around organising everything.

'Yes,' Colin told her. 'I have nothing else to do but look for your cat. My goodness, you all think I am here just to do everything. Can you all do nothing for yourselves?'

'Are you going to be looking?' Val asked, trying to ignore that Colin looked like he was having some kind of nervous breakdown.

'Yes, I will add this to my ever-growing list of things to do. Now you just go and leave it all to me.'

Val headed up to her room.

'Colin! Where are you?' came a voice echoing down the castle corridor.

'Elizabeth, what do you need?' he shouted back, eager to please her.

'Yes, Elizabeth,' he added.

'I heard that Val has a problem and you were not keen to help her,' Elizabeth said.

'Oh no, I am happy to. It's just that I have so much to do.'

'Well, that's not what I have been told. It seems you are being awkward.'

'No, not at all. Everything is okay. I will have Magnificent found in no time,' Colin replied.

'Okay. I did not think you would have been like that,' Elizabeth said. 'Anyway, that old cat is in the main hall beside the fire, and it has gone white. I would go and help him as fast as you can, Colin, and take Alex with you. For some reason he seems keen to help you.'

While Magnificent had been sleeping in front of the fire, the chimney had been cleaned and the fireplace reset to ensure the room was heated for the night. The crew had washed down everything and put the fire on. This heated up, and Magnificent was now not only covered in sea salt but soot. This combined to create a suit of hardened mess.

Alex and Colin entered the main hall, where Magnificent was now completely white. The sea salt and soot had made him as stiff as a board. They and the construction crew could hardly hide their laughter.

'Check him out,' came the calls. 'It's a statue of an old smelly cat. No, I have it. He's a saltshaker, he comes complimentary with every function. We could just put him on the main table.'

All were falling over with laughter. Poor old Magnificent had managed to bake himself while sleeping by the fire. Colin looked at Alex and both fell about laughing at this little white statue motionless by the fire.

'Are you in there?' Colin called to Magnificent.

'Yip,' he squeezed out, trying as hard as he could, his jaws hardly moving at all.

'Can you move?' Colin asked.

'No,' came the reply from Magnificent.

'Shall I get Alex the eagle to take you to your room, Magnificent?'

'Yes,' came another one-syllable reply.

And so Alex the eagle, still trying his very best to stop laughing, carried the salt statue up to the room.

Bang! came a noise from the front door. As Val opened it, Alex was making ready to use Magnificent to bang on the door again.

'Stop it! No using my Magnificent to bang on the door,' Val shouted at Alex. 'Bring him in before you hurt him. Put him over there and get out of my room too. Another thing, please stop that laughing at him. He is very sensitive.'

Val looked at her furry friend and ran a big bath. Magnificent hated baths. This was going to be a struggle of epic proportions, and Val hoped the winner would be one clean furry friend. Mind you, for once Val had the upper hand. It was not as if Magnificent was going to run off.

'Now, Magnificent, I need to put you into the bath,' Val told him. 'So be brave and let's do this.'

She stooped to pick him up. He must weigh about 150 kg, or 23 stone. She was unable to lift him.

'Oh no,' she thought. 'What now?'

Then there was a bang at the door. She turned to Magnificent.

'You stay there.' Then she laughed. 'Of course, you're going to stay, you can do nothing else.'

Val went to the door.

It was the instructions being delivered for tonight.

'Can you place it over there?' she asked.

'Of course, no problem,' Colin told her. He looked at the situation and asked Val if she would like a hand.

'That would be very nice, but no laughing at my pussycat. He is very sensitive, you know,' Val told Colin.

Colin promised, and both tried to pick up the statue known as Magnificent. They tried as hard as they could but were unable to move him.

'Is he digging his claws into the floor?' Colin asked.

'Yip,' Magnificent called out.

Val shouted at him and then told Colin to go and get Alex.

In came the eagle and all of them tried once again. No way were they moving him. He stuck his claws into the ground as hard as he could. They all went outside the room so Magnificent would not hear them.

'I have an idea. Maybe we could take him outside. We could get a hose, and even if he does not move that will not matter,' Colin told Val.

They went back into the room, watched by Magnificent, his eyes following them.

'Right, turn on the hose,' Colin said. Alex held it towards the statue and the water started to flow. Colin grabbed Magnificent and Val managed to put this most grumpy cat into the bath.

They all ran as Magnificent once again made a bid for freedom.

But at least, Val told Colin and Alex, he could move again. Hopefully that grumpy wee cat would clean up.

Chapter 7
Dreams Realised

'It's time, Magnificent, old friend. Let's go, Rodney, and bring the two spare broomsticks.'

It was about 10 p.m. as they entered the great hall, and it looked amazing. The chandelier glittered and the long tables had been set up with the finest crystal glass. Val and her friends were greeted at the door. She was the very last to arrive. The hall was full.

Colin quietened the room and then announced Val to the great hall.

'It is with great pleasure we proudly present Val Witch from Fortingall village. Val has invented broomsticks that have transported our kind by air for the first time.'

With that, the room erupted into cheering and clapping from all the other tables. Tweet stood up at the very top table, and all the others in the hall also stood.

The great hall was filled with all the potential winners of Witch of the Year, and the ceremony was about to begin. The Great Gathering would also begin.

Tweet stood up to speak.

'It gives me great pleasure, firstly, to welcome all of you to this Great Witches' Gathering. This is going to be very special.

A big thanks to Colin. You have done a fantastic job introducing all our guests and nominees, and the great hall has never looked so good.

It is our intention to inaugurate the winner of Witch of the Year into the Great Council of Witches. We, the council, have concluded that we need to have some fresh witches sitting with us at the top table. And for the first time in our history, this will take place.

I will now present a list of great deeds and inventions the Great Council have decided are worthy of consideration. We will also, of course, be hearing words from our Great Coven of Witches' leader. After consideration, we will, with great sadness, say goodbye to our leader and choose another.

This will, of course, be done after the normal reflection period, and it is down to the Great Leader to decide who is chosen next.

Now, without delay, I introduce you to Heff of Brechin Rugby Club for inventing the never-ending glass.'

The crowd went mad. They loved this, and the rugby team's reaction was truly something to see. Heff stood up, barely able to make himself heard above the noise, and started to speak.

'Well, I spent years of my life studying the whole art of food and drink. In inventing this I knew the pleasure I could bring to the world. Nothing in the world means more to me than supplying help to others. Thank you all.'

Tweet thanked Heff for a wonderful speech.

'Now welcome Hiver of Crows Pass, Albury, New South Wales, Australia, for his great deed of finding out just the right number of spells to liquid needed to cure the terrible disease of liars.'

Hiver then told a long story about life where so many had lied and cheated their way through, causing much misery to others by their actions.

'Gone should be the days of us all accepting this, and it is my hope truth should always be told.'

'Well, that was good news for us all,' Tweet told the hall. 'Now on we go to the next. Val Witch from Fortingall, for inventing a broomstick that flies.'

Val explained how she had invented this to help her kind simply get around.

'It was hard and took time and a great deal of effort. It taught me that all are valued, no matter how small or large. Without help from everyone I could not have achieved anything. I have been truly humbled by the support and help from all of you.'

'Well,' said Tweet, 'those are our three nominees that we have for you all, and indeed for all around our known places. Would you now welcome your Witches' Council: Aliya, Mila, Varvara, and of course Sophia.'

The hall erupted into cheering and shouting for their favourite invention or deed. In the crowd a kangaroo and a wombat from Albury in New South Wales were cheering. They loved it. They were interviewed by the news team from Witches Live at Nine.

'Well, just who are you here to support?' the reporter asked.

'Why,' Ned the wombat told them, 'I feel that Hiver is without doubt the best.'

And the big red kangaroo, called Marlu, who was apparently very famous, said, 'I must admit I like the idea of the never-ending glass, mate. This could stop pubs running out of beer, which would keep my dad happy.'

The reporter tried to move away from him as she was, well, afraid. Ned and Marlu moved back to the bar, both now arguing that you should not have mentioned someone else's invention.

'I mean, we are only here because of Hiver,' Ned told Marlu.

'You fool,' Ned added, but Marlu was having none of it.

'It's boring. Look at that bunch over there, they are having great fun.'

Next, the reporter went to Magnificent.

'Well, who do you think is going to win?' she asked, trying to get away from the argument. But still Ned and Marlu were having none of it. Eventually, the reporter snapped at them.

'Well, normally you would support who you came with,' she told Marlu.

'Really,' Magnificent replied. 'I suppose you would think that. Anyway, goodbye. I think Marlu and I are going to see if we can find something fun to do.'

'She was a bit rude,' Magnificent said to his new best friend Marlu. 'Check out that old witch over there, she has fallen asleep.'

Magnificent and Marlu now made their way over to poor old Sheila. She had just retired and was happily sleeping, bothering no one.

'Let's see what we...'

At that, Sheila woke up.

'Just think about this, you two. It's been a while, but I am certain I am more than a match for an old cat and an overexcited kangaroo. Believe me, you really do not wish to even think it.'

Magnificent thought to himself how good she was.

'Well, we are pleased to meet you.'

'And I you,' Sheila told Magnificent. 'Now you two had best be on your way, I think.'

Sophia stood up to speak. She was the most elegant of all the witches' council. When she stood, all returned to their tables and looked towards her.

'Dreams, hopes, and those who have devoted so much of their lives to improving ours. They bring us such joy and happiness. Not one of them is a loser. We must all celebrate their endeavours. With this, I ask all the nominees in this year's Witch of the Year to stand for a moment. Heff, Val, and of course Hiver, please, everyone, give them a big cheer.'

'Heff, your invention of the never-ending glass was most welcome in relieving thirst in our world. We hope you manage this,' Sophia told the crowd. They cheered and clapped. 'Brechin Rugby Club, I believe your nickname is the Bruce, are thanked for their support.

'Hiver,' exclaimed Sophia, turning towards him. 'Your single-minded progress in the pursuit of the truth has been inspirational, and the research that led you to this most splendid piece of work. Stopping lies is a truly inspired piece of work. Please show your appreciation, for this is truly a great achievement. I congratulate Albury, New South Wales, for nominating Hiver to us.'

The crowd cheered and clapped. Marlu and Ned were so proud of Hiver that they asked him to speak. He stood up and told them he had nothing to say but thanks to all for being there for him.

Sophia then tells all that the final nominee was Val Witch.

'You have transformed the way we travel. Bringing new lands and opening the world to all of us with a Broomstick that flies. I have one myself and must say just how much it has changed my life. Such devoted belief that you could achieve is fantastic. You accepted help and gave help. To the good village of Fortingall, thank you for nominating Val Witch. Val, do you wish to say anything?'

Val stands up to say a few words.

'This feels so unbelievable that I am here. However, the happiness I feel is also filled with sadness at Bert the Brave not being here. Magnificent, my loyal friend, and the faithful people of Fortingall for putting up with us and nominating me. Without encouragement from others nothing is possible.'

The Billylows & The Fisherman - Band

Sophia thanks Val and then points to the open fire and shouts,

'You are on fire! Someone get a hold of that cat, put out the fire!'

Magnificent looks around him, bewildered. He had been happily toasting himself in front of the open fire. Everyone runs towards him, throwing bucket after bucket of water over him. He is soaking.

It turns out he was not on fire at all. It was steam rising from his wet fur after his bath. He is very angry and runs off. Val runs after him and just catches him before he leaves the castle.

'First little Bert the Brave and now you. Come back, let's finish this. I will rub you dry with a towel, and we could go back in no time.'

Just at that, Rodney comes out.

'You two need to hurry up. You will not believe what's going on in there.'

Chapter 8
You Never Can Tell

Once again, they all ran into the hall. By this time the band had started up. Billy Low and the rest of the fishermen were playing some good tunes and everyone was up dancing. It was some very strange dancing, but if you had more arms than legs or whatever, it was best just to shake them down anyway.

'Look,' Rodney shouted. 'Just look over there. It's Bert the Brave! Told you!'

He shouted back to Val and Magnificent. 'He has made it.' And with that he decided to fly over to see him. Rodney, as we all know, is fantastic at flying, but landing? Well, he had not quite got the hang of that yet. In fairness, he was getting better.

Before anyone had a chance to stop him, he was airborne and flying directly at the top table where Bert the Brave was speaking with the Witches' Council. Over the heads of everyone, then a sharp right, nearly hitting the band. He flew on, cheered by all. Perhaps they did not fully understand that this was not going to end well.

Rodney, excited at seeing Bert the Brave, went even faster. Why not do a quick round-the-room flight, he thought. His speed was well past thirty miles per hour and the crowd were spinning in circles to watch. The band played faster and faster; Rodney was now the star attraction.

Val screamed, 'Rodney, now slow down!' But he was so happy. The crowd cheered ever louder and the band played even faster.

'Look at this, Val. It's amazing, truly great fun!'

Magnificent and his new-found friend Marlu were now very dizzy, as was everyone and everything in the room.

'Why is he doing that?' Marlu asked Magnificent.

'Not a clue,' came the reply. 'But it's time we found a place out of the way, under a table or something.'

They ran for cover as Rodney completed his sixtieth lap. Still the band played ever faster and the crowd cheered ever louder.

Magnificent shouted to Bert the Brave. 'Take cover, he's coming to see you!'

Marlu was trying to fit under the smallest table, his head and tail sticking out, with his wombat friend Ned running over everything and everyone to get to cover beside him.

But Billy Low and the fishermen played on, thinking this was maybe something witches did as part of the Gathering. Billy told the band to hurry up.

'Speed up, this must be part of the celebrations. Play faster!' he screamed.

Val screamed once again, but no one could hear her above the noise of the band and the screaming crowds. Rodney was now off course and completely out of control. Magnificent looked around at the chaos, thinking that Val was now going to be in deep trouble as the Witches' Council were staring directly at her.

Sandy and Ian, two very big eagles, were placed beside Val. Alex stood behind her, with Colin looking on at the increasing mess.

A voice was then heard to say the simple word, 'STOP.' Everything did so, and Rodney was suspended in mid-air, as was everything else.

Time itself had been stopped by something. Sandy, Ian, Alex and Elizabeth, who had joined them, were not. Nor were the top table.

Aliya of the council spoke. 'What really have you done, Val? That broomstick. It must be completely...'

'Well,' Val began. 'Well, he does get a little excited.'

'Really,' Varvara shouted. 'We hadn't noticed.' They all looked around at the mess. 'You, Val, have done this. He belongs to you and therefore it's your fault.'

'To be honest,' Val said, 'broomsticks really have a mind of their own and are technically not owned by anyone.'

'What?' Varvara screamed. 'You dare to answer back to the Witches' Council?'

Val tried once again to explain but was asked not to. She tried again and was silenced by Varvara.

'Well, it's true,' Val once again stated.

'Not another word, Val,' Varvara said. 'Just not one. Bring that mad cat here.'

Sandy went to the table where a seemingly lifeless Magnificent had been frozen in time. They sat him down and, with a small gesture, he was awakened to this most serious situation.

'Magnificent,' Elizabeth called out gently, 'come on little one, time to wake up now.'

He was bewildered as he was put next to Sophia. Sophia asked him if it was true that broomsticks had a mind of their own.

'Well,' he told them, 'I have not a clue.'

Sophia told him it was important. 'Magnificent, do broomsticks have a mind of their own?' she asked once again.

'Not a clue,' Magnificent replied. 'Sorry, I really don't know.'

Poor Val was in big trouble. The Witches' Council looked to be in no mood to put up with this. But in fairness to Magnificent, he had realised that Rodney the broomstick's fate was also in the balance. If he said that broomsticks had minds of their own, then Rodney would face the consequences.

'Stop this,' said Mila, the last of the Witches' Council members to speak. 'We should try this. I mean, it's close to midnight on the 31st of October and that's when we can awake the two new broomsticks, is it not? We will find out then if it's true.'

'Good thinking,' Sophia said. Val reminded them that broomsticks decide if they wish to be with you, or not, as the case may be.

'Val, you are in no position to tell us anything now, are you?'

'Well, that's not true. I know more about this than you all do. And another thing, it's not my fault or Rodney's that this has happened. He is just a little highly strung, that's all. So, if that clears this up, I will just be on my way.'

Varvara told her, 'Nice try, but you are going nowhere till we figure this out.' She then turned to Magnificent and asked him to explain what he thought about all this.

'Well, it's a bit like potty training, it's hit and miss,' he told Varvara.

All the witches just stared at him and moved on.

'What about the fact we have still to present the trophy and Bert the Brave? This is a mess, just a big mess. We should speak to him. Where has he gone?'

Rodney - The Broomstick

Magnificent was now wondering just what, and who, they were talking about. Could it be Bert the Brave was also in trouble? He looked around the hall at all the figures frozen in time. He saw his friend Marlu still under the table, or more accurately with the table on top of his body, and Ned below him. Rodney was still in the air, but there was no sign of Bert the Brave.

'Well, let's sort this out. We cannot hold up time forever,' Sophia told them.

Sandy, Ian and Alex then asked if they were still to watch over Val.

'Yes, keep a good watch over that one and of course that cat.'

Elizabeth decided that they needed to speak to the Boss now. She shouted at Colin, and he was off to find the Boss.

Magnificent looked at Val and she gave him a reassuring smile, then told him, 'We have faced worse than this.' But truthfully, even Val could not remember when.

Time and the room were completely still. It seemed so long ago since Rodney had been flying around creating mayhem. Val sat waiting for the Witches' Council to decide what was going to happen next. Her dreams were all but gone now. Val had concluded that they were not going to give her anything. No trophies, no membership to the Witches' Council, because they might not even get back to the Great Caledonian Forest. All hopes and dreams were gone.

'They are coming, I can hear them,' Magnificent told Val. 'Look over there, just at the small entrance. Can you see?'

Colin walked in, followed by a small figure, a very, very old leaf bug slowly making its way towards them.

The Witches' Council all knelt together, showing their respect for what seemed to be the Boss.

The leaf bug was still so far away that Magnificent could not make out very much. But really, was this small bug the Boss? Surely not. It just could not be. Both Val and her loyal cat must have been thinking the same thing as they turned to look at each other. Val spoke first.

'Really, Magnificent, you think that's the Boss, or is it another trick?'

Magnificent had not a clue what to think. 'We had better not do anything else to upset them, I think.'

'Well,' the Boss now spoke, 'quite an eventful day, I think. Never have I had such fun. You Witches' Council look to be very worried about something. Come forward and explain what has gone wrong.'

The lights were very low, and the Boss looked like just a shadow peering out towards them.

'Well...,' Varvara started to explain.

The Boss asked once again, 'I asked what has gone wrong?'

Varvara composed herself and spoke. 'Rodney the Broomstick has tried to smash up the whole Gathering on the instructions of Val

Witch of Fortingall. The broomstick, travelling at over sixty miles per hour, circled the room causing much distress and dizziness. He looked at one point as though he was going to attack you.'

The Boss then turned to look at Rodney, released him from frozen time, and demanded an explanation.

Rodney looked up, then towards Val and Magnificent, telling them he was so sorry for being out of control. He was stopped by Varvara and told to respect the Boss and answer immediately.

'Well,' Rodney told the Boss, 'I saw my friend, who I thought had been upset because I was unable to find him. Being delighted that I had found Bert the Brave, I just had to go to him. So I went outside to tell Val and Magnificent that Bert the Brave had turned up. We all went back into the castle. Then I spotted what I believed to be Bert the Brave sitting at the top table with the Witches' Council. I flew towards the top table in a roundabout way, I guess.'

'Okay, thank you for your honesty,' the Boss told Rodney.

'Magnificent, please will you now tell us what you think happened?'

'Well,' Magnificent began, 'the whole thing is really my fault. You see, I was going to leave after someone from the Witches' Council had water thrown over me. So I went outside the main hall to leave but was stopped by Val.'

The Boss stopped him and asked if he knew which Witch had asked that he be covered in water, and to please point them out.

'It was that one,' he said, raising a paw towards Sophia.

Sophia, startled at this, told the Boss that the crazy cat was on fire.

Magnificent then shouted, 'No, I wasn't. I was minding my own business, getting dry from the bath that Val had forced me into.'

The Boss then asked Magnificent if it was just steam.

'Yes,' Magnificent replied.

'Well, a simple mistake. Please, Sophia, apologise for this act. Even if you meant well, I still think you need to let this poor victim know you meant no harm.'

Sophia stood up and walked over to Magnificent. She gently and very quietly apologised to him, scared stiff as she had never been so close to feeling like someone was going to do her harm. She knew a Witch's anger was something to avoid at all costs.

'There now, does that feel better?' said the Boss.

'Okay, Val,' said the Boss. 'Time for you to tell me what happened.'

'Well, it's just as has been said. I didn't tell Rodney to smash anything. Please continue with what happened.'

'Okay, Rodney came to me and Val saying that we would not believe what was going on inside the castle. Val persuaded me to go, and we went in.'

The Boss then asked Magnificent, 'So at no time did Val tell Rodney to cause damage? I mean, just look around us. The place has been smashed up.'

'Not sure,' Magnificent replied, still aware that both Rodney and Val were in deep trouble.

'Okay,' the Boss told Magnificent, 'I understand you are smart enough to realise that someone is going to be blamed and you don't wish to be the one pointing the paw at them. But you must realise that I have the power to punish all of you. So once more, did Val tell Rodney to smash the place up? And the truth, please.'

Magnificent looked first at Rodney and Val, both now terrified, then at the Boss.

'No, I never heard Val tell Rodney to smash the place up.'

'Thank you, please sit down, Magnificent,' the Boss told him.

'I would never have done anything to stop the Gathering, Boss. Honest,' Rodney told the Boss.

The Boss then looked at the three of them and turned to the Witches' Council.

'Have you anything to add?'

'Well,' Varvara said, 'just look at what they have done. Someone must be blamed. It's not fair after so much work.'

'I understand,' the Boss told them. 'Now feelings are running high, as you all suspect this has stopped the Gathering and that Rodney and Val are to blame.

'You have permission to extend frozen time until I have made my judgement,' the Boss told the Witches' Council. He then told the others to leave the room, saying this should not take long, as the Witches' Council needed to discuss it.

'Well, it's clear to me there has been much misunderstanding, and that Rodney was just over-excited. What do you all think?' the Boss asked them.

'Really, I mean he has single-handedly smashed up the entire hall, and the Gathering is now left in the biggest mess we have ever had,' Varvara said. 'I simply don't believe that old Witch is really the kind we would like in the Witches' Council, do you?'

Aliya spoke up. 'I don't think this is so. Rodney and Val never intended this. I must say that we should put back time and let's say to where we already know what's going to happen. We could put it right, making it look like it was just you and that famous thing you do.' She turned to the Boss.

'Sophia, your option is?' the Boss asked.

'Well, not certain. It doesn't look right, but it's hard to tell. What does everyone else think?'

'Sophia,' the Boss told her, 'I never knew why I chose you to be a part of the Witches' Council. You are so indecisive. Come to think of it, Varvara, you always seemed too harsh, and Aliya, you seem just too soft, but you always have good and wise choices for me to make.'

'Mila, you are my most trusted of all. I should be sure to go with your recommendation.' And to be fair, the Boss normally did.

Val and Rodney awaited their fate, and poor old Magnificent could do nothing to help them this time.

The hall was dark, and the Boss came out of the shadows once again. You could not really make out what the Boss was.

Mila spoke to them first.

'Rodney, you are special and the first of your kind. I have nothing but admiration for you. You must, however, learn to control yourself. Do you understand?

'Val, you clearly had nothing to do with this, and we think that perhaps you could be part of the solution to Rodney's problem. You found a way to let him fly, so you may well be the one to help him make good and safe landings.

'The Boss has therefore ruled that you will train him and have one year to complete this, or Rodney will be banned from flying forever.

'As for the damage, you can all get stuck into cleaning up to allow us to get on with the rest of the Gathering. Make a good job of it, and we will leave you in the running for Witch of the Year. Do you have any questions? Are you all clear on what is to happen now?'

All remained quiet, so Mila told them to get a move on, as they needed to get time moving once again.

The Boss had said nothing, and none of them had seen him. Elizabeth and Colin told Magnificent and the eagles to help clean up the hall. Rodney swept as fast as he could, and Val tried hard not to get on the wrong side of the Boss, realising just how close they had all come to goodness knows what. The Witches' Council were not known to tolerate things going wrong. The hall was ready, and a plan was made so no one would know anything had happened.

'First, Alex the Eagle will lift Rodney back into the air, and we will slow him down to a point where he can land without crashing.

'The band will stop playing for a few seconds while he lands, and you will all start to cheer. Stand next to that crazy rugby team. They cheer at everything.

'All ready?'

Mila counted them in, and all was then back to normal.

Chapter 9

And Finally

Once again, the Gathering was underway. None of the guests suspected that they had been frozen in time. The hall looked stunning once again, and the band, Billy Low and the Fisherman, were playing their hearts out. They sounded terrific as Rodney was brought to earth gently and without any incident at all.

The Great Gathering was brought to silence by Varvara of the Witches' Council.

'Well, what a night. To Billy Low and the Fisherman, might I say, "all these years of travelling in that whale have made you into the best band I have ever heard." You may all go back to the Strathelliot, your beautiful ship, and remember not to let Shawna the whale need to help you again. As you know, she can be a wee bit overprotective. You no doubt do not wish to spend the next twenty years travelling the world, do you?'

Billy respectfully agreed, and he and his band headed towards their ship, the Strathelliot, which Shawna had given back after so many years. The parting words of Varvara rang in their ears. She had told them the band was the best anyone had ever heard.

'Your band, Billy Low and the Fisherman, will forever hold a place in our hearts. Please can we have a massive cheer for the band, Billy Low and the Fisherman.'

Billy's crew asked if they could stay to see what happened next. Billy asked, and was told, 'Most certainly, you can.'

At those words, a massive cheer went up from the whole hall.

'Now it is time for us to reveal the Witch of the Year. To present this, we have the Boss. So please put your hands, feet, or indeed everything you have together, and let us make the Boss feel welcome.'

The lights were dimmed, with only one beam of light from a spotlight cutting through the dark. The crowd remained quiet, excited about the prospect of finding out what was going to happen next. Who was going to win? This was the highlight of the whole Gathering, and the atmosphere was electric.

Then the top table was lit up to reveal the Witches' Council: Aliya, Mila, Varvara, Sophia, and of course, sitting in the middle was, as if by magic, a very small but perfectly formed leaf bug called Bert the Brave. He was, in fact, the Boss, appointed about ten thousand years ago. He had never told anyone, as he had never seen the point. This allowed him to live as he pleased, and to be fair, that was mostly what he did.

'What did they say?' Magnificent asked Val. 'Did they say Bert the Brave?'

'I could not hear with all the noise,' Magnificent told her, 'but you might be right. I think they did say that.'

Val turned to Magnificent, completely stunned, thinking this must be some kind of trick.

'I think I heard that Bert the Brave is the Boss.'

'Me too,' Magnificent told her. 'Me too.'

Looking completely stunned, Val thought, what kind of trick was this? Surely this could not be. Bert the Brave was now seated in the middle of the top table, and still Val and Magnificent could hardly believe their eyes.

Then came a tremendous noise. The whole castle shook, and the very ground moved beneath them.

'Well, that has done it for me,' Magnificent told Val. 'That really is Bert the Brave.'

Rodney was beside himself. 'See,' he shouted. 'I told you. That is why I was so excited and flew around the room. Look, it is Bert the Brave. It is him. He is still alive, and he is the Boss. Look, it is really him.'

The crowd were ecstatic. This was the Gathering they all loved. The excitement and the dramatic ending were now going to happen. Bert the Brave, the Boss, began to speak.

'You are the best, all of you. None better than anyone else. We live in harmony as it is handed down in the great dreamtime.'

Bert the Brave had the crowd cheering. The excitement was too much for some, and they had to be helped.

But on with the speech. Bert the Brave continued.

'All of you know that being at one with all is what we strive for. But each year we choose the outstanding and celebrate the achievements they bring to us. This year will be different, as we will be adding to the Witches' Council.'

The Media Mafia, three strange large stones given life in a freak accident by Bert the Brave many years ago, fell off their seats. To be fair, this had nothing whatsoever to do with anything, but the resulting bangs added to the occasion. The three of them rolled off to report the day's events. Bert the Brave looked at them rolling away and told the crowd to look out in case the Media Mafia should crush them. Then he said, 'Let us get back to this.'

'From this day on, Heff, you are part of the Witches' Council.

'Hivers, from this day onwards, you are now part of the Witches' Council.

'Val, you are also now part of the Witches' Council.'

Bert the Brave went on to explain that the need to ensure that new ideas and new ways of thinking about everything had always been part of all of them. 'We learn,' he said, 'as Val the Witch demonstrated, not from what we have already learned but from our mistakes and efforts to learn why we failed. This inspires us to try harder and to follow our own path to succeed.

'Heff, Hivers, and of course Val have proven they never give up, and whatever happens only makes them more and more determined to invent and succeed.

'And so, it is with great pleasure that I introduce to all of you our three new Witches' Council members.'

This had never happened before. The crowd were shocked. Normally one was chosen to join, and sometimes no one was chosen at all. Three in one Gathering was extraordinary.

Bert the Brave then told all three of them, 'Please understand that it is your duty to be at one with all and uphold the values of this Council: honesty, integrity, fairness, and respect for all things.

'You three shall now stand for the Land, Sky, and Water, until the end of time itself, encouraging all to live in harmony with all within the Universe, from which all is both given and taken away.'

Bert the Brave then turned to face the new members and told them they must now accept by a simple yes or no. This would form the oath of allegiance to the Witches' Council.

No one in all history had refused to join the Witches' Council. It had never been refused. However, the words must be said, and the answer to the question given.

'Val,' Bert the Brave asked. 'Do you accept? Please tell me yes or no.'

'Yes, I do,' Val told him.

'Heff,' Bert the Brave asked. 'Do you accept? Please tell me yes or no.'

'Yes, I do,' Heff told him.

'Hivers,' Bert the Brave asked. 'Do you accept? Please tell me yes or no.'

'No,' Hivers replied. 'I cannot say that I think I am worthy of this. I do not think that I have done enough to justify this.'

The crowd were stunned by this but were told by Bert the Brave that all must respect the choice of Hivers.

'We will have a small break while I speak in private.'

Bert the Brave then went with Hivers to a small room.

Hivers looked at Bert the Brave, afraid that something bad was going to happen. Bert the Brave quietly explained why he had chosen him and why he felt it was so important that it was accepted.

'You, Hivers,' Bert the Brave explained, 'are worthy, and being inducted into the Great Witches Council is so important to me and to all. If I was to give you some time to think about this decision, would this help?'

Bert the Brave then asked Hivers why he felt unable to join the Witches Council.

Hivers the Platypus asked how much time would be given to decide.

'As much as you need. You are going to be a part of the Witches Council, and so we will wait until you feel ready, or not, as the case might be. Being on this Council is very important to me, but your doing this of your own free will is even more important.'

'Then I accept,' Hivers told Bert the Brave, 'on one condition, if possible.'

Bert the Brave looked puzzled but asked, 'What would you like?'

Hivers went on to explain.

'When growing up no one used Boondaburra, which is my correct name, and this made me sad and unconfident. They called me Hivers as I liked to speak a lot. Being honest, not much of it made any sense to anyone but me, but I never deserved being called Hivers.'

Bert the Brave smiled and told him,

'Boondaburra, if this is what you wish to be called, then that will be. Even if you decide that you don't wish to be part of the Council.'

'Now will I ask Boondaburra to join the Witches Council?' Bert the Brave asked.

'Yes, I would like this very much,' came the reply from Boondaburra.

'Very kind of you. Shall we spread the good news to the Gathering?' Bert the Brave said.

A very excited Boondaburra told Bert the Brave that this new beginning was going to be great and that now and always it would be his life's work to ensure the very best for the Witches Council.

'Good,' Bert the Brave replied. 'Let's go and get back into the Great Gathering to let everyone know this great news.'

Bert the Brave now told all at the Gathering that Hivers was now to be known as Boondaburra and nothing else would be acceptable under any circumstances.

'We are now going to ask Boondaburra once again to join the Witches Council.'

'Boondaburra,' Bert the Brave asked, 'do you accept? Please tell me yes or no.'

'Yes,' Boondaburra replied.

The three of them would now be part of the Witches Council.

'So can we have a great big cheer for our latest members!'

At this the crowd started clapping and cheering. The noise was deafening.

'Good,' Bert the Brave then told the crowd. 'And now that we have our new Witches Council, let us come to the matter of the Witch of the Year. We need to choose for the following reasons: improvement to our world, care and attention to the environment for the betterment of all.'

Bert the Brave turned to Heff.

'You have won, and it gives me the greatest pleasure to introduce you all to your Witch of the Year. Water gives life and is one of the fundamental elements that make up our very world. Inventing the Never-ending Glass that stays full always will lead to many having a future that otherwise might not have had one. Congratulations, Heff. We are all very proud of you.'

'Now we come to the sad ending of my leadership. It is time for me to live out my life in the company of my old friend Dave in the Great Caledonian Forest.'

Bert the Brave told the Great Gathering that the next Boss would be Val Witch.

'I realise that Varvara and Sophia will be disappointed, but I hope they will help Val as much as they have helped me. Beginning next year Val will be given all my powers. Next year's Gathering will be held for Val, and please let's all welcome and accept her.'

The atmosphere at the Gathering was electric, with the members of the Witches Council looking on to see if Val would accept the offer.

'Val Witch, please kindly tell us your answer to being the next Boss.'

Bert the Brave and the entire Gathering now awaited.

Val Witch stood up and spoke to the entire Gathering. Bert the Brave had Sophia hand over the words that must be spoken, smiling towards Val as she passed them.

'Can I have a moment?' Val asked.

Bert the Brave requested that the band, Billy Low and the Fisherman, play some songs to entertain everyone while the Witches Council spoke to Val.

Bert the Brave asked the entire Witches Council to join Val and him in the room at the back.

Heff, Boondaburra, Aliya, Mila, Varvara and, of course, Sophia gathered around with Bert the Brave. Val sat at the round table looking at them all.

'Are you all completely certain this is the correct decision, and no one wishes to question or reconsider it? I mean, I have only just become a member of the Witches Council.'

Bert the Brave began to address Val and the Witches Council.

'It is hard to make such a decision, but it must be made. Looking to the future for the benefit of all, Val, in my opinion, is by far the best to succeed me as the Boss. However, we have always tried to be fair-minded and open within the organisation, and so at this point we should have a vote.

'All here will indicate and show whether they wish, or indeed decide against, Val being the new Boss.'

'Heff, how do you say?'

'I agree, Val.'

'Boondaburra, how do you say?'

'I agree, Val.'

'Aliya, how do you say?'

'No, I don't agree, Val.'

'Mila, how do you say?'

'I agree, Val.'

'Varvara, how do you say?'

'No, I don't agree, Val.'

'Sophia, how do you say?'

'No, I don't agree, Val.'

'Val, you as a member are, of course, entitled to vote. How do you say?'

'No, I don't agree.'

'Now, at this point, as the Boss, I am able with a casting vote to say that Val will be made the next Boss, but it is my feeling that this would cause disharmony within the Witches Council.

'I propose this. Val will, of course, remain as one of the Witches Council but will have to complete a walkabout journey in which Val will deliver a gift that I have long been meaning to present. It is my hope that once everyone sees just how well Val performs, we will reach agreement that Val then becomes the next Boss.

'Boondaburra, you are to be with Val, and Val, you may take whichever others you feel necessary.'

All at the meeting agreed to this and praised the great wisdom. Tweet was then called in to record the outcome.

He asked, 'What are we to call Val?'

'She will be called Val Witch until, or if, the position of Boss is given. Once it is given, Val will be given the name of Valarie the Brave in line with the Witches Council.'

'Until this day comes, I will hold the post of Boss. Are we all clear?'

'Yes,' came the reply, and Bert the Brave then asked that all return to the Gathering.

The end until the next time that is.